"Let me tell you my dream."

Peter reminded himself to breathe. "Please do."

"It's a real dream." Harper ducked her head. "I mean, it's not a wish or a fantasy, it's something that comes to me while I'm sleeping. Over and over."

With no idea where this might be heading, he merely waited.

"I'm out in a field." Harper studied her clasped hands. They were pretty hands, with long tapered fingers and lightly polished nails. She'd moved her wedding ring to the right side, he noted. "There are two boys playing. Sometimes they're toddlers. Other times, they might be five or six."

"Two boys?" he repeated.

A quick nod. "There's a shadowy figure playing with them. A man, but I can't make out his face. They're playing catch, or tag—it varies."

"I see." But he didn't.

"Nobody realizes I'm there, and I think that's because I'm not." Although tears glittered on her lashes, Harper met Peter's gaze squarely. "I have the sense that I'm meant to give them life. That's all. They won't be *my* sons. They're supposed to be born and I'm supposed to make that happen."

"And let them go."

"Exactly."

Dear Reader,

Not many years ago, the notion of achieving parenthood through egg donations and surrogates lay in the realm of science fiction. Today the opportunity exists for a widower like high school biology teacher Peter Gladstone to have longed-for children.

No wife? At Safe Harbor Medical Center, that's no obstacle. A fertility issue of his own? No obstacle there either.

But Peter does have one problem: choosing the woman who will be the genetic mother of his child or children. Although all the donors at Safe Harbor have been screened, she'll still be a stranger.

When an unexpected opportunity presents itself, he's torn. Harper Anthony, a nurse who's the widow of a former colleague of Peter's, is listed among the donors. She's attractive, intelligent and a wonderful mom to her six-year-old daughter.

If he picks her, is it ethical to keep his identity a secret? Perhaps so, except that he's teaching her daughter in a summer sports program and keeps connecting with Harper. The closer they become, the stronger his dilemma.

I hope you'll join Peter and Harper, and share their journey with them!

Best,

Jacqueline Diamond

His Baby Dream

JACQUELINE DIAMOND

HARLEQUIN® AMERICAN ROMANCE®

Recycling programs
for this product may
not exist in your area.

ISBN-13: 978-0-373-75458-8

HIS BABY DREAM

Copyright © 2013 by Jackie Hyman

All rights reserved. Except for use in any review, the reproduction or utilization of this work in whole or in part in any form by any electronic, mechanical or other means, now known or hereafter invented, including xerography, photocopying and recording, or in any information storage or retrieval system, is forbidden without the written permission of the publisher, Harlequin Enterprises Limited, 225 Duncan Mill Road, Don Mills, Ontario M3B 3K9, Canada.

This is a work of fiction. Names, characters, places and incidents are either the product of the author's imagination or are used fictitiously, and any resemblance to actual persons, living or dead, business establishments, events or locales is entirely coincidental.

This edition published by arrangement with Harlequin Books S.A.

For questions and comments about the quality of this book, please contact us at CustomerService@Harlequin.com.

® and TM are trademarks of Harlequin Enterprises Limited or its corporate affiliates. Trademarks indicated with ® are registered in the United States Patent and Trademark Office, the Canadian Trade Marks Office and in other countries.

Printed in U.S.A.

HARLEQUIN®
www.Harlequin.com

ABOUT THE AUTHOR

The author of more than ninety romances, mysteries, Regencies and paranormals, Jacqueline Diamond lives in Orange County, California, with her husband of more than thirty years. Writing about a fertility program at a medical center draws on Jackie's long-standing interest in medicine, which began when her father, then the only doctor in the small Texas town of Menard, delivered her at home. You can learn more about the Safe Harbor Medical series at www.jacquelinediamond.com and keep up to date with Jackie at her Facebook site, JacquelineDiamondAuthor.

Books by Jacqueline Diamond
HARLEQUIN AMERICAN ROMANCE

Chapter One

Glancing up from his clipboard across the shouting, seething crowd of children and parents half filling the community college gym, Peter Gladstone spotted the woman with an eerie jolt of recognition. For an instant, the entire scene froze.

Taller than most of the moms, she moved toward him with easy grace, her soft, short chestnut hair framing an animated face. His chest squeezed. She reminded him so much of Angela.

Jerking himself out of his daze, Peter noted the little girl hanging on to her left hand and the little boy trying to pull free on the right. "Can I help you?" he asked as they reached him.

"I'm sorry to bother you, Peter." From her tone and use of his first name, she obviously knew him. And he *had* seen her before, so why couldn't he place her? He certainly ought to remember a woman who bore such a marked resemblance to his late wife. Perhaps he'd met her last summer here at Safe Harbor Sports Camp, but he had a strong sense that he knew her from somewhere else.

"It's no bother." He strove for polite words to obscure the fact that he'd forgotten who she was. "The first day is always chaotic."

"It sure is a madhouse." Up close, she had beautiful

green eyes and a smile that hinted of mischief. "Must be tough adjusting to all these little kids."

"It's quite a change." For most of the year, Peter taught high school biology, as she apparently knew. During the summers, he earned extra income as assistant director of this sports program.

Mercifully, a name on the clipboard jumped out at him. Mia Anthony, age six. The listed parent was Harper Anthony. Occupation: nurse. Now he placed her—the widow of Sean Anthony, a fellow teacher with whom he used to coach wrestling after school. Her appearance had changed in the past few years, he reflected, studying her.

"It's the hair," Harper said.

"Excuse me?"

"You were trying to place me. I just got my hair cut," she explained. "Used to be long."

"I remember." *Finally.*

Behind her, a woman approached with a little girl. "Bathroom?" she inquired frantically.

He pointed toward the exit. "Down the hall on the right."

As they departed, Peter gazed around the room, making sure the college-age counselors were correctly grouping the kids under the banners marking off the grade levels. Kindergarten through second-graders were assembling by the bleachers on one side, third- through fifth-graders on the other and sixth through eighth under a basketball hoop.

The camp had been established for dual purposes. It gave college students summer jobs working with kids, developing job skills and preparing for careers in education. It also provided half- and full-day programs that kept children active during the vacation months.

"Reggie, hold on!" Harper tightened her grip on the little boy. "This is Reggie Cavill. He's the son of a friend. Well, the nephew, actually—long story. Anyway, Adrienne works an overnight shift so I brought him this morning. I want to be sure he's registered."

"Did his aunt complete the form online?"

"I think so."

Peter found the name Cavill, Reginald, on his list, along with his age, five, and Dr. Adrienne Cavill, obstetrician, listed as guardian. "Everything's in order."

"I was wondering if he and Mia could be placed in different groups." Harper shook her bangs out of her eyes. "They're almost like brother and sister, so they tend to squabble."

"Thanks for letting me know." He jotted down the information. "We do divide the kids into smaller groups for some activities. I'll make sure they're separated."

Reggie stopped squirming to stare at Peter. He was a cute little guy with short blond hair and two missing teeth. "Are you, like, a coach?"

"I am," Peter said. "Do you have a favorite sport?"

"Eating," Mia piped up. "And smearing it all over his face."

"Shut up!" The little boy feinted around Harper and gave her a shove, which Mia deflected with a well-timed turn of the shoulder.

Catching the boy's arm gently but firmly, Peter drew him away. "At sports camp, treating other people with respect is an important part of athletics. We don't hit, push or kick."

"She made fun of me!"

Peter fixed Mia with a serious expression. "When we treat people with respect, they respect us in turn. So we don't use insults, either."

"Even if they're true?" she asked.

He fought to hide his amusement. "Even if we *think* they're true."

"Thank you." Harper regarded him appreciatively. "It's hard for kids to grow up without a father. Being here will do them good."

"I'm sure it will." He watched her shepherd the tykes, each with a backpack in place, to their assigned group.

It was kind of her to help a friend's little boy. Single parents had to band together, especially if they didn't have close relatives in the area. Peter was grateful that his mother and father lived only half an hour away, since he was contemplating single fatherhood himself.

Suddenly he remembered where he'd seen Harper Anthony recently. Or, rather, seen her photograph.

This evening, after camp, he resolved to take another look. Because today's chance encounter might turn out to be the answer to a very important question.

HARPER ALMOST WISHED she hadn't run into Peter Gladstone that morning. Although of course she'd noticed his name on the sports camp website, she hadn't thought much about it until she'd stood right in front of him.

His sheer physicality had caught her off guard. That incredible build. Those bright blue eyes. The confident way he held himself. The leashed strength in his voice.

Since her husband died in an off-road vehicle accident three years earlier, Harper had avoided situations that might tempt her to get involved with a man. She didn't need the complications and had no interest in remarrying.

Although her very normal needs had a way of surfacing, as they'd done today, she recognized the less enjoyable side of involvement, at least for her. Organizing her life around a man, tailoring her activities to his preferences— that might have suited her as a teenager, when she'd first fallen in love, but she was twenty-eight now. And enjoying the chance to live the way *she* wanted.

Still, suppressing her instincts must have made her vulnerable. Even in that noisy gym, she'd had to struggle to project calmness and control.

Her reaction was ridiculous, Harper reminded herself later as she weighed the next obstetrical patient and escorted her to an examining room. During their marriages, there'd never been any vibes between Harper and Peter Gladstone. He'd seemed devoted to his wife, and while Harper had liked Angela's sweet personality when they ran into each other—mostly at school functions—she'd found the woman rather passive.

Nothing like Harper's outspoken, strong-willed friends. Nothing like the self-reliant woman Harper was determined to become, either.

After several years of financial and emotional struggles, she was finally getting her life on track. Five months ago, she'd landed this job as a nurse assisting Dr. Nora Franco in the medical office building next to the hospital. A couple of months later, she'd moved from an apartment into a house where her daughter could have a pet, and now she'd chopped off the long hair that Sean used to love.

She valued the freedom to experiment and make her own choices. What she didn't need was a guy who, judging by the wife he'd chosen, preferred compliant women.

"You got your hair cut." The patient, Una Barker, a heavyset woman in her seventh week of pregnancy, sat on the edge of the examining table. "It's flattering. Practical for summer, too." She wore her own reddish-brown locks short and tightly curled.

"My daughter's hair kept getting snarled." Harper attached the blood pressure cuff. "She refused to cut hers unless I did the same, so here we are. Frankly, I wish I'd done this years ago."

"I hope one of my twins is a girl," Una said. "But I'll be happy as long as they're healthy."

Harper moved to the computer terminal to note Una's blood pressure, which was slightly elevated but within the normal range. "Any problems? Nausea? Back pains?"

"A little queasiness."

"Is it bothering you now?" The patient might need a few crackers to hold her until lunch. The office kept a supply.

"Not at the moment." Una indicated a pile of garments at one side. "Should I change into one of those lovely hospital gowns?"

Harper chuckled. While the thin, ill-fitting robes served their purpose, no one liked them. "Not today. Dr. Franco just wants to see how you're feeling." Having achieved the first successful pregnancy in Safe Harbor Medical Center's new egg donor program, Una merited extra attention. Also, carrying twins added to her risk. "She should be in momentarily."

"Wait—unless you're in a hurry?" Una interjected.

"Not at all." Casual conversations allowed patients to bring up symptoms or issues that might otherwise be overlooked. "Is there something else?"

"I hope you don't mind if I ask how it's going with you," the patient said.

"With me?" Harper repeated.

"Stacy mentioned that you were approved as an egg donor." Una had achieved her pregnancy thanks to a donation from Harper's close friend and former roommate Stacy Layne, a surgical nurse. Stacy, who'd accidentally become pregnant with triplets the same month as Una, kept in close touch with her fellow mother-to-be. "Have you been chosen by a couple yet?"

"Not yet. I've only been on the registry for a week." The application process had taken several months while Harper underwent medical tests and a psychological evaluation. "I hope the mom and I can be friends like you and Stacy." Although some parents, and some donors, preferred to remain anonymous, Harper had offered to meet potential recipients in person.

"The preparation really brings you together," Una said. "I mean, coordinating your menstrual cycles—how personal can you get?"

Harper was looking forward to the experience. She hoped someone chose her soon. "Stacy says she feels closer to you than to her own sister." Harper didn't have a sister, just an older brother who lived in New Mexico and hadn't even friended her on Facebook. So a sisterly relationship would mean a lot.

"Our kids will be half siblings." Una shifted position on the table. "I'm glad they'll grow up together."

"You can move to a chair if you'd be more comfortable." Harper reached out to help her down.

The patient waved her off. "No, thanks. So, will you tell your little girl about the kids, if—when—there are any?"

"I've already talked to Mia." Harper believed in open communication, to an age-appropriate degree. "She understands that I have this little boy in my dreams. Two of them, actually. It's like they want to be born. Since I have no desire to marry again, this is a way to give them life."

"That's so sweet!" Una declared.

"Plus I love the idea of helping another family." Harper didn't mention money, since that wasn't her primary motivation. The five thousand dollars she'd receive when her eggs were harvested would go straight into Mia's college fund. Some donors earned more if they were willing to travel to be near the recipient or if they were recruited because of a special characteristic, such as a genius IQ.

A tap sounded on the door. "Ready for me?" Dr. Nora

Franco, a blonde who seemed unaware of her movie-star looks, peered in at them.

"Just talking about kids," Harper told her.

"My favorite subject." Nora had an eighteen-month-old son with her husband, a police detective.

"Nice talking to you, Una." Yielding her place to the obstetrician, Harper scooted out.

As she went to summon the next patient from the waiting room, Harper basked in a warm glow, thinking about rescuing those little boys from her dreams. What a miracle if someday they might run and play for real.

THE FIRST DAY OF SPORTS camp, as Peter had discovered the previous year, brought its share of bumps. Homesick kids, conflicts and acting out, youngsters with a fear of water who resisted swimming, and disorganized parents who arrived late—all were par for the course. It was nearly 7:00 p.m. by the time he collected his car from the faculty parking lot and drove home.

Although this northern part of Safe Harbor, California, lay several miles from the ocean, a sea breeze drifted through his car window. On his left lay a light industrial area, with a shopping plaza on the right. A note clipped to the dashboard reminded Peter to stop for milk and cereal. In his impatience, he ignored it. He had enough supplies to last until tomorrow, anyway.

A few minutes later, he reached a neighborhood of old-fashioned cottages set amid palm trees, firs and jacarandas. Angela had fallen in love with the name of their street, Starbright Lane, even before she saw the fairy-tale cottage with its gingerbread trim, broad front porch and latticed windows.

While Peter might have preferred a modern design, he'd been relieved to discover they could manage the payments on their teachers' salaries. Room for a home gym, along with a small paved basketball court behind the double-wide garage, had sealed the deal for him. After three years of cramped apartment living, he'd been grateful for the space.

From the garage, Peter carried his laptop case through the connecting door to the green-and-white kitchen. Glass-front cabinets displayed Angela's flowered dishes and tea-cups, while the scents of vanilla and orange spice lingered even now, nearly two years after her death. He half expected to see her turn from the stove, greeting him with a smile. Teaching first grade hadn't dissuaded her from cooking a full meal almost every night, while Peter had handled dishwashing duty.

After setting down the laptop, he cut through the living room to fetch the mail from the front-porch box. Since he did most of his banking and bill paying online, there wasn't much beyond advertising flyers.

Peter tossed those in the trash and strode down the hallway, past his bedroom and the guest room that they'd planned to convert into a nursery. A knot formed in his chest.

They'd tried to start a family for over a year before consulting a specialist. As one of six children, Angela had expected to conceive easily, and they'd attributed the delay to stress from her busy schedule.

Maybe if they'd gone in earlier, they'd have caught the ovarian cancer soon enough to save her life. The symptoms—bloating, lower back pain, persistent lack of energy—had been so vague that even Angela's regular doctor hadn't found them alarming. Only later had they learned that one of her grandmothers had died of ovarian cancer, and an older sister had been diagnosed with breast cancer in her twenties but survived.

Six years of happy marriage had been followed by six

months of suffering and pain. Hope would flare at word of an experimental treatment, only to fade. Peter still had trouble believing he'd never again hold his loving wife in his arms.

Only recently had he followed up on another discovery they'd made during their fertility workup: his low sperm count. The doctors he'd originally consulted hadn't been able to pinpoint the problem. Then, recently, he'd contacted men's fertility specialist Cole Rattigan, who'd diagnosed Peter with a rare allergy to his own sperm.

According to Dr. Rattigan, his condition shouldn't stop him from becoming a father. Via a high-tech medical procedure, doctors could inject his sperm directly into an egg.

The chance to cherish a son or daughter from infancy filled him with excitement. He could hardly wait to shower a child with love, and to see the light of understanding dawn as words and concepts became real to that tiny new person.

Peter's parents, retired teachers who also lived in Orange County, supported his plans. His sister, a lawyer who lived in Maryland, enjoyed her high-power career and didn't want kids, so when he'd informed his parents of his intention to become a single father, they'd been thrilled. His child or children would grow up with loving grandparents, family holidays and the security of being part of an extended family.

In the den, he opened his laptop and grumbled at the slowness with which it booted up. As soon as it did, he navigated to the fertility program's website and entered his password.

Despite his eagerness, he went first to the roster of surrogate moms. Dr. Rattigan had suggested that, as a legal precaution, Peter use both an egg donor and a separate surrogate. That way, the woman carrying the baby wasn't giving birth to her own genetic child and, if she changed her mind about relinquishment, had no legal grounds for claiming custody.

He'd already chosen the woman he would employ, a married homemaker and mother who, during a previous surrogacy, had given birth to a healthy baby girl. Peter reviewed Vanessa's description and photo, which showed a friendly woman with strawberry-blond hair, above the caption I Love Being Pregnant!

When he'd interviewed her, he'd been impressed by her enthusiasm and good nature. He had no doubt she'd nurture his child, providing a loving start before birth.

The most difficult decision lay ahead. Previously, while studying the profiles of egg donors, he'd been keenly aware that he was choosing a woman to provide half of his child's genetic makeup. Her personality, her intelligence, her strengths and her weaknesses would strongly influence his future child. While Peter believed in the importance of the home environment, there was no denying the role of heredity.

Unable to make a choice, he'd postponed the decision. Then, today, he'd seen Harper Anthony.

Clicking on the section that listed egg donors, he found her photo at once. The first time he'd viewed it, he'd experienced a vague sense of familiarity, and assumed he must have seen her around town. He hadn't connected the woman identified only as Mrs. H.A. to his late colleague, nor—given her sweep of long hair—had he been struck by the resemblance to Angela, although he could see it now.

Why was she willing to do this? Peter wondered. Her statement contained the usual remarks about wanting to help others, loving children and treasuring the miracle of life. Perhaps working in the medical profession had influenced her decision.

She offered to meet with prospective recipients. How awkward would that be? Besides, having a woman he knew as the egg donor was asking for trouble, Peter conceded. They would no doubt continue to run into each other after the child was born, and what mom could resist feeling possessive toward her genetic child, even though she hadn't carried it in her body?

Yet he'd observed what a caring mother Harper was, and he'd taken an immediate liking to her outspoken, bright little girl. This way, his child's background wouldn't be such a question mark.

He wouldn't have to inform her. He'd been assured that he could maintain complete confidentiality if he chose. With the surrogate, that hadn't seemed important—indeed, Peter wanted to experience the pregnancy with her, to view the ultrasounds and to hear his baby's heartbeat—but the donor would be out of the picture once the pregnancy became established.

Still, he'd see Harper around town, and he didn't like keeping her in the dark. Moreover, as the years went by, she might learn he'd had the child with a surrogate, notice the resemblance and put the pieces together.

Peter took another look at the woman in the picture. Her skin glowed, and her delicate necklace resembled a daisy chain. The impression was natural and healthy, which matched the woman he'd seen today.

Troubled, he closed the site. He'd hoped to make a decision. Instead, he'd simply raised new complications.

Well, he'd only decided a little over a month ago—once he received his diagnosis from Dr. Rattigan—to proceed with becoming a father. Peter had quickly passed the screening process and background check required by the hospital's surrogacy program. Now he faced one of the most important decisions of his life.

He'd have to think about it.

Chapter Two

Mia was jumping up and down, her tennis shoes springing off the living room carpet. "Hold still," muttered Harper, taking aim with a brush and achieving only a passing swipe at the messy honey-colored strands.

"Good thing you cut her hair," observed Stacy, who looked feminine and comfortable in a peach knit top and maternity jeans. Only halfway through the first trimester, her pregnancy was already beginning to show, since she was carrying triplets. "It's adorable even when it's rumpled."

"I'm going to Disneyland!" the little girl crowed. Although she'd been to the amusement park in nearby Anaheim before, it never lost its appeal.

"And we appreciate your keeping us company." Stacy's fiancé, Dr. Cole Rattigan, grinned with anticipation. He had honest brown eyes and a sturdy build that he maintained by bicycling to and from the hospital almost every day.

"I'm sure the park will be full of kids." Harper set the brush aside. "Saturdays in summer tend to be jammed."

"That's half the fun. Anyway, we want to experience this through her eyes," Stacy said. "It'll be years before our kids are old enough to go on rides. And with three of them, I doubt *we'll* have a chance to relax and enjoy it."

"My first trip definitely requires a kid." Having moved to Safe Harbor from Minneapolis the previous year to head the men's fertility program, Cole evidently hadn't found time until now for the county's best-known tourist attraction.

"Mia, stop jumping! This isn't sports camp." Harper restrained her daughter before she crashed into the dark-wood entertainment center.

"We'll be honing our parenting skills," the surgeon added. "This is as much a learning experience as a pleasure trip."

While that might seem an odd attitude, Harper had grown accustomed to Cole's refreshingly naive view of personal interactions. Brilliant in his medical practice, he'd only recently emerged from an emotional cocoon after falling in love with Stacy. Raised by a surgeon mother who'd purposely chosen an uninvolved father, he'd missed out on many of the usual childhood rituals, such as birthday parties and trips to theme parks. "I wish you'd at least let me pay for her ticket."

"It's her birthday present," the doctor responded cheerfully. "Besides, we like spending time with Mia." He and Stacy had babysat previously, allowing Harper to attend a seminar on digital photo editing.

"Her birthday isn't for two weeks. But thank you." Harper took a final peek inside Mia's backpack. Additional sunscreen, tissues, a water bottle, school ID and the cell phone that doubled as a camera. Everything checked out.

As her friends escorted the bouncy girl to their car, Harper stood in the doorway of her ranch-style home. Around the front steps, geraniums, miniature roses and marigolds brightened the flower bed, and the scent of jasmine drifted from a neighbor's yard.

As for Mia's upcoming birthday, Harper hoped the Disneyland visit might compensate for what she feared would be a lackluster party. She couldn't afford a costly celebration like some of her daughter's school friends had thrown, with hired entertainers or a trip to see Cirque du Soleil. The rent on this house already strained her budget.

The car vanished down the street. Harper stood for a moment longer, letting herself adjust. As much as she relished a rare free day, it felt weird not to have her daughter with her.

She went inside for her camera. As a teen, in addition to shooting for the high school website, she'd taken pictures for the sheer pleasure of seeing the world afresh. Since then, she'd been too busy to do more than record key events. That was changing, however.

Harper packed snack items, applied sunscreen and set out extra food and water for Mia's black-and-white kitten. Then she locked the house behind her with the buoyant sense of going on a holiday.

Rather than take her car and have to pay attention to driving, Harper strolled a few blocks to the bus stop on Safe Harbor Boulevard. En route, she paused to photograph a spray of yellow blossoms on a tree and a climbing rose blooming across an arched trellis. Typical of early summer weather in Southern California, the sky was overcast. That would burn off later, but for now a breeze cooled the air.

Slowly, she relaxed into an easy rhythm that contrasted with her usual hurry. A whole day to take pictures. How precious was that?

On the bus, a family clustered with a large picnic basket. A group of girls chattered and laughed, while a young couple sneaked kisses. After observing her fellow riders, Harper turned to gaze out the window, studying shapes and patterns of light and shadow.

They rolled past stores, offices and the occasional bicyclist on a trail that paralleled the boulevard. Off to the right Harper glimpsed the six-story medical center and the adjacent office building where she worked.

Even though she'd loved being a full-time mother, Harper treasured her life now. It was busy, yes, and demanding, but she and Mia had a lot of freedom. If she didn't feel like cooking, they ate sandwiches and salads for dinner. On weekends, they took spur-of-the-moment trips.

Harper had never experienced this kind of independence before. Stunned by her father's death in a car crash when she was sixteen, she'd clung to her boyfriend, Sean. She'd leaned on him through college and their four-year marriage, adapting her interests to his. Hiking and motorcycle riding—until her pregnancy—had replaced photography, and being a wife and mother had replaced nursing. She'd had no idea to what an extent her reliance on him had preempted her sense of self until after his death.

Although Harper would always treasure their years together, she didn't care to repeat the experience with anyone else. Today, she felt liberated.

When the bus crested a rise, before them spread the U-shaped harbor from which the town took its name. Small boats and a scattering of yachts lined its edges, while sailboats and catamarans headed toward the jetties that protected it from the Pacific Ocean.

Along a harborside quay lay shops and a café. Farther down the shore, past the yacht club and some private waterside homes, Harper noted beach umbrellas and blankets staking out areas of sand. So far, however, only a handful of wet-suited surfers braved the chilly waves. It was always colder at the ocean, even compared to a few miles inland.

Zipping her jacket against the wind, Harper descended at the bus stop and made her way onto the beach. No one seemed to mind when she captured their images: an older couple holding hands as they strolled, a man tossing a beach ball with his little boy, a woman in a floppy hat pouring a steaming cup of liquid from a thermos. Thank goodness for memory cards that stored thousands of images.

A clump of palm trees framed the subtle colors of sea and sky. Walking and clicking, Harper lost track of time—a rare luxury. As the day warmed, she removed her jacket and tied it around her waist.

A man caught her eye—a muscular fellow, head down, wind ruffling his hair and sweat darkening his T-shirt as he jogged toward her along the sand. Athletic shorts emphasized his sculpted thighs and, admiring the classic impression of masculinity, Harper snapped a couple of quick pictures.

Then his chin lifted and familiar blue eyes met hers. Startled, Harper lost her grip on the camera, which was saved from a fall by the cord around her neck. At the same time, the man slowed.

"Peter. Uh, hi." She debated whether to apologize for photographing him, but that might require an explanation. And her only reason had been that she found him attractive.

Breathing hard, Peter halted in front of her. Since their conversation the previous Monday, Harper had glimpsed him several times at sports camp. He'd always been surrounded by mothers asking questions about their children and sometimes, judging by their body language, flirting with him. Who could blame them?

He indicated the camera. "Is this for a project?"

"Nothing in particular." In his presence, Harper instinctively tossed her hair, only to find that she missed the accustomed weight of it. Anyway, she didn't mean to react with flirtatious moves like those other women. "Photography used to be my hobby. I'm rediscovering it."

"Mind if I take a look?"

"Not at all." Harper switched the camera to display mode and handed it over.

Peter leaned toward her as he flicked through the pictures. "You have a terrific eye."

Shifting closer to see the shots, Harper caught the appealing scent of clean male sweat. "Isn't that a cute little boy? Something about him reminded me of…" She broke off.

"Of Sean?" he asked.

Harper examined the image. "Not really. Just—oh, it's not important." She wasn't ready to share her dream about little boys.

He shifted away. "Mind if we walk? I'd like to keep moving while I cool down."

"Sure." Glad of the company after a morning alone, Harper fell into place as they strolled toward the pier. She adjusted her stride to his without difficulty, since he was only a bit taller than her five foot nine inches.

"Where's Mia?" he asked.

Guiltily, Harper realized that she hadn't thought about her daughter in over an hour. Still, she'd resolved not to be a helicopter parent, and Mia could reach her by phone if necessary. "She went to Disneyland with my friend Stacy. It's her fiancé's first visit and they thought it would be more fun with a kid."

A Frisbee flew toward them from a group of teen boys. Peter caught it easily and skimmed it back. "You don't worry about her?" Quickly, he added, "Not that you should."

"Stacy's a nurse and her fiancé's a doctor, so she's in good hands," Harper said.

The crowd on the beach grew thicker as they approached the pier, forcing them to weave around sunbathers and picnickers. "Want to grab a bite at the café?" Peter asked. "I don't mean to interrupt your photo session."

"Oh, the light's too harsh now, anyway." Harper laughed. "That was rude, wasn't it? Like I'd only join you because the light's bad for picture-taking."

Peter unfurled a smile. "I appreciate the frankness."

"I'm sure Angela was *way* more tactful." She halted, regarding him apologetically. "I'm running off at the mouth."

"Nothing wrong with talking about Angela." Peter held out a hand to help her up some large rocks that abutted the pier. "I mentioned Sean, didn't I?"

"I guess you did." His grip sent prickles along Harper's arm. Reaching the wooden quay, she released his hand quickly.

They strolled past boat slips and, on the inland side, boutiques selling beachwear, surfboards, hats and anything else a tourist might buy. At the Sea Star Café, they were lucky enough to snag a booth by the window.

"I'll get the food," Peter offered, since the café served from the counter. "What would you like?"

Harper handed him a twenty-dollar bill. "I'll have a cranberry muffin, a blueberry muffin and a cup of chai, and don't even try to pay for it."

Peter's eyebrows drew together. "Okay, but—is that what you're eating for lunch?"

"Why?"

"Not exactly a balanced diet."

"Don't tell me you're a health nut." She bristled at the idea of someone dictating what she ate. This was *her* free day.

"No, it's just that as a…" He floundered for a moment. "I figured that, as a nurse, you'd be a stickler for nutrition."

"Sean used to get on my case about carbs," she responded testily. "It was all protein and vegetables with him. I'm making up for lost time."

"Okay, okay." Peter raised a hand placatingly. "Just asking."

Harper hadn't meant to start an argument. By the time he returned, carrying a tray between the crowded tables, she regretted snarling at him. "Thanks, Peter. I'm sorry about biting your head off."

"I can take it." He set her cup of tea and the muffins in front of her.

"Usually I eat healthy stuff, but today when Mia isn't here, I don't have to act like a grown-up."

"No explanation necessary." On his plate rested a whole-wheat pita sandwich bursting with sprouts, hummus and lettuce. "I wasn't trying to control you. That's what comes from being a teacher, I suppose."

"Especially a biology teacher?" she teased.

"I'm glad you equate that with healthy habits." Peter took his seat. "Some women draw other conclusions about my expertise in biology." His cheeks reddened. "Man, that came out wrong."

"Good thing this isn't a date," Harper told him. "Just think of me as Sean with, well, a few distinctions."

"I'm trying *not* to think about those distinctions." He turned an even brighter shade. "Seriously, I don't know where this stuff comes from."

"Most men wouldn't apologize, they'd move in for the kill." Harper had fended off more than a few piranhas, including men accompanying their pregnant wives to Dr. Franco's office. She felt sorry for any woman married to a creep like that. "Um, as long as I have your attention, can I pick your brain?"

"By all means." He regarded her over the pita.

"I'm planning a birthday party for Mia that won't cost much." As they ate, Harper explained the situation, concluding with, "Any ideas about what I could do in my backyard?"

She wasn't sure why she expected a childless man to come up with an answer. Still, as a teacher and a sports camp leader, Peter had experience with groups of kids, Harper reflected as she watched him study the sailboats in the harbor. It was hard not to sneak glances at his appealing profile.

And hard not to notice that he's all guy. Confident, physically attuned men drew her, and Peter had that in common with Sean. Like Sean, he was also a little domineering, she reminded herself. It wasn't a bad trait, just unsuited to her.

Clear blue eyes refocused on her. "My personal philosophy is Never Miss a Chance to Teach."

"Even at a birthday party?"

"The average backyard is a paradise for biologists." Pushing aside his empty plate, he planted his elbows on the table.

The only backyard biology that occurred to Harper involved a shady bower, protective bushes and activities wildly inappropriate for a children's party. However, they'd already dismissed that topic, and thank goodness.

Hoping her thoughts didn't show, she said, "I could put them to work planting a vegetable garden. Adrienne did that last spring when she was watching Mia and Reggie. My daughter swears they dug for hours, although mostly I think they played in the dirt."

"Might be kind of messy for a party," Peter said.

"I agree. What else did you have in mind?"

"Bugs." He gave the word a lilt, as if it ought to pique her interest.

"Spoken like a biology teacher." Nevertheless, Harper supposed bugs might make an interesting theme. In her experience, kids seemed to love eating Gummy worms and chocolate mud pie cupcakes. "I could design invitations and decorations on that theme," she mused. "It wouldn't be hard to come up with bug-related games, either."

"If your backyard is like most people's, I'm sure you can find anthills, ladybugs and spiders." Peter's face lit up with enthusiasm.

"You mean, real bugs?"

"Magnifying glasses should make good party favors."

That did sound like fun, if handled right. "What would the kids do?"

"Spot bugs and identify them," Peter said. "In the process, they'll learn about the creatures that share our lawns and homes."

"Our homes?" Harper shuddered. "Not mine, thank you."

"Even in a clean house, you'll find tiny spiders, and if there are spiders, they're eating something," he observed. "Plus our clothes and sheets are loaded with microscopic dust mites."

Harper raised her hands. "Too much information."

"Sorry." Peter ducked his head. "I get carried away."

"Let's keep the bug hunt outdoors." Harper sighed. "If Mia thinks our house is full of bugs, she might have trouble sleeping."

"Good point." After a moment's reflection, he asked, "When's the party?"

"In two weeks," Harper said.

"I could stop by and check your yard before then, if that would help." His eyes shone at the prospect. "But I don't want to impose."

"Impose?" She'd welcome the assistance. "Anything you can do would be great. When's a good time?"

"How about tomorrow afternoon?"

She hadn't expected such a quick turnaround. "I promised my friend Stacy to go shopping for her wedding gown." Although the event wasn't until September, it could take a while to find the right dress. "How about next Saturday?"

"Two o'clock?"

"Great." Had she really just invited Peter to her house? But they would have a chaperone. "Mia will be delighted to see you. Although she's a little nervous around spiders." *As if I'm not.*

"She's a cutie." Peter seemed to relax at the mention of her name. Apparently he hadn't been trying to get Harper alone, not that she'd figured he was. "By the way, spiders aren't insects."

"What are they?"

"Arachnids."

Harper made a mental connection, not to biology but to a mythology book she'd read to her daughter. "Like Arachne, the weaver."

"Exactly. You'd make a good teacher." Coming from Peter, that was high praise.

"Thanks." As they arose and cleared their plates, Harper added, "I'll text you my address. Although I guess you have that already, at camp."

"I'm sure we do." He kept his tone politely impersonal. "However, I don't consult school records for my personal use. We should exchange numbers."

"Good idea." They clicked to the contacts section on their phones and input that information for each other.

Judging by his tone and body language, he intended to

keep their relationship platonic. Despite a small, rebellious twinge of regret, that suited Harper fine.

AT HOME, PETER CLICKED open the egg donor website. There she was, the woman with whom he'd eaten lunch. Viewing Harper this way felt sneaky, but how could he tell her what he was considering?

Surely no etiquette book addressed the issue of what a man might discuss with a friend on the subject of choosing her as an egg donor. If he decided against it, she might feel rejected. If he chose her, well, what then?

He'd felt more comfortable talking with Harper today than he'd felt with any other woman since he lost Angela. There'd been none of the usual awkwardness when women flirted with him. Since he became a widower, several female acquaintances had invited Peter to dinner but he always made excuses. Others came right out and told him that, after more than a year, he ought to be dating again. They strongly implied that he should start with *them*.

While he appreciated the compliment, he didn't like being pursued. When he and Angela met during their student teaching, they'd gravitated together instinctively.

Like Harper and me?

Peter *did* find her appealing. However, that might result partly from her resemblance to Angela. Plus, having acquaintances in common and a shared history helped the conversation flow.

Well, he'd volunteered to drop by her house next Saturday. With a little more contact, surely he'd be able to decide whether to select her as the mother of his children, or move on to another candidate.

Chapter Three

"Tell me again how blue his eyes are," teased Stacy, fingering the lace on a tiered, strapless gown.

Embarrassed, Harper glanced around the bridal shop. Luckily, none of the other customers appeared to be paying attention. "I showed you his picture already!"

"And tell me how helpful he's being about the party."

"Change the subject."

"Okay." Stacy stretched. "It's amazing how sore I am from walking around Disneyland. That was so much fun! Thanks for loaning us Mia."

"I'm glad she didn't drive you crazy."

"Not at all."

Yesterday's outing, from which they'd returned about 10:30 p.m. after the fireworks, had left all parties exhausted. Today, even the usually meticulous Stacy had smudged her eyeliner and stuck a headband over her loose curls.

Harper had barely dragged Mia out of bed this morning in time for church. Afterward, she'd dropped off her daughter to spend the afternoon with Adrienne, who'd set up a pretend medical clinic for Mia's and Reggie's teddy bears. "Oh, darn!" Stacy made a face as another woman corralled the tiered gown. "I think that was the only one in my size."

"You should have let the saleslady set it aside," Harper said.

Stacy pretended to glare. "See how much sympathy you get from me when you're shopping for your wedding to Mr. Blue Eyes."

"Quit that." Harper would have given her friend a light shove, had Stacy not been pregnant.

"Kidding aside, it's the first time I've seen you like a guy since Sean." Stacy lingered in front of a display of hats and veils. "Aren't these cute?"

"Pick the dress first," Harper advised.

"But someone might take the prettiest hat!"

"You'll want a veil."

"Why do you say that?" her friend demanded.

"Because you're the veil type. Or the something-romantic type. Not hats." Having shared an apartment with Stacy and been friends with her since junior high, Harper knew her taste ran to the ultrafeminine. "Trust me."

"I do." Stacy sighed. "Which is lucky, because Cole can't help me choose a dress, or colors, or a cake. He's a sweetheart but when it comes to girl stuff, he's hopeless."

"Your sister would be ideal." During their teen years, Harper had seen how talented Ellie was at designing and sewing clothes. Now, married with four kids, Ellie lived in Salt Lake City and, with their mother, ran a boutique that sold stuffed animals in custom outfits. "Too bad she lives so far away."

"She gets final approval over the bridesmaid dresses." Stacy held up a sleek off-the-shoulder satin gown. "Along with you."

"That makes sense." Harper had been invited to be maid of honor, with Ellie as matron of honor. While unusual, the arrangement suited the small church setting and the fact that Cole, new to the area and with no close relatives, had only two groomsmen: his boss, the intimidating Dr. Owen Tartikoff, and Cole's male nurse, Lucky Mendez.

"My feet hurt. I have to sit down." As Stacy sank into a chair, the saleslady hurried over, asking if she was okay and offering tea, which they gratefully accepted.

"That's another problem with choosing a gown," Stacy murmured. "By September, I'll be sticking out to here. Possibly out to *there*." She indicated a point halfway across the room.

"We have designs with plenty of room," the clerk assured them.

"For triplets?" Stacy asked.

After a blink of surprise, the saleslady said, "I'm sure we can accommodate you."

Soon Harper and Stacy found themselves in a large dressing room with a selection of gowns, along with bridesmaid dresses in Harper's size. Since Stacy hadn't yet chosen her colors, the options were wide open.

"Pregnant brides must be fairly common," Harper commented as she helped her friend into a dress with a forgiving waistline.

"Yeah, but I'll bet none of them got pregnant the way I did." Stacy smoothed out the skirt. "When you take those hormones and they tell you to watch out after they harvest the eggs, they aren't kidding."

"So I hear." As part of her preparation to become an egg donor, Harper had been warned that the harvesting process didn't catch every egg. Donors were strongly advised to abstain from intercourse for the rest of that cycle or risk getting pregnant with multiples.

After Stacy donated eggs to Una, she'd believed her period had started. That same night, celebrating her birthday, she'd had an unexpected romantic encounter with Cole. Initially, she'd planned to give up the babies for adoption, but despite Cole's clumsy approach to wooing, he'd eventually won Stacy's heart.

"You and Una inspired me," Harper added, "but that doesn't mean I intend to follow *all* your examples."

"Good." Turning to examine the back of a dress, Stacy paused as her gaze met Harper's in the mirror. "Maybe I shouldn't say this…"

"When has that stopped you?"

Her friend smiled. "Okay. I'm glad you'll be helping a family have children…"

"But?" Curious, Harper slipped out of a pink dress that was too pale for her complexion.

"When Una called to say she was pregnant, I thought I'd be ecstatic." Stacy eased out of her gown, as well. "Instead, I felt as if the bottom had dropped out."

That puzzled Harper. "Why?"

"I didn't understand it," Stacy admitted. "You know, the program initially tried to reject me as a donor because I hadn't had a child of my own. I browbeat Jan until she agreed." Jan Garcia, R.N., headed the egg donor program.

"It upset you when Una got pregnant?" Harper prompted.

"I felt empty." Stacy drooped at the memory. "My arms ached to hold those babies. Although I was ashamed of my reaction, that's how I felt."

"I wish you'd told me." If Harper had known Stacy was struggling, she'd have been more supportive. Not that she'd been unkind, but she *had* been distracted by her new job and Mia's needs. "Since I already have a child, though, my arms won't be empty."

"What about those little boys in your dreams?" Stacy reminded her.

"I don't see them as mine." Harper had discussed the matter with the program's psychologist. "They're separate people who deserve their own lives. I'm just helping them."

"That's what *I* thought about my future babies," Stacy cautioned.

"And now you get to watch Una's twins grow up," Harper pointed out. "Plus raise three of your own."

"You're missing the point," Stacy pressed. "I just want you to understand that things might not go as planned."

"I appreciate the warning." Harper hadn't meant to dismiss her friend's concern. "But while I'd love to share the recipient's pregnancy and birth, I accept that that might not happen. In the meantime, what do you think?" She twirled in a light purple dress with blue trim. "This is pretty."

"It fits beautifully."

"Could you go for these colors?" Harper would be able to wear the cocktail-length dress again, a definite plus in view of the price.

"Oh!" Stacy eyed the dress in dismay. "Ellie said any color but puce."

"This isn't puce. It's purple. What color *is* puce?"

"I'll check." Sitting on the bench, Stacy consulted the dictionary in her phone. "It says here it's dark red. I always thought puce was purple."

Standing upright to avoid wrinkling the dress, Harper searched on *her* phone. "This site says it's a grayish red-violet." The color displayed was lighter and more muted than the one she wore.

Stacy continued doing research. "Listen to this! *Puce* is a French word that refers to the color of bedbug droppings."

Together, they said, "Eww!"

"I'm sure the bedbugs have been out of the picture for hundreds of years," Stacy said.

"Do you suppose that's why Ellie hates the color?" Harper asked. "Or does she loathe anything purplish, reddish or violetish in general?"

"Violetish? Never mind." Stacy pressed a number. A moment later, she said, "Ellie? What color is puce?"

Over the phone, which was on speaker mode, came, "It's yellow-green."

Stacy and Harper laughed.

"What?" squawked Ellie's voice.

"I'll tell you later," Stacy promised. "What do you think of this dress?" She held up the phone so her sister could see. Harper twirled like a model.

"Ooh, cute!" said Ellie.

"You like the color?"

"You bet!"

They agreed to have one sent to her in her size. With Ellie's and her mom's needlework skills, they could tailor it as needed.

Stacy hung up. "I can't believe we agreed on the bridesmaid's dress *and* my colors. Purple and blue. How cool!"

"You still haven't found a gown," Harper warned.

Stacy indicated the remaining dresses. "If I don't find one today, it won't be the end of the world. We've got months and months."

That turned out to be a good thing. None of the gowns caught the bride's fancy.

Only later, after they'd purchased the bridesmaid gowns and Harper had been measured for alterations, did Stacy's words come back to her. *I felt as if the bottom had dropped out.*

Before volunteering, she'd searched the web for comments by egg donors. Some *did* have regrets, but most reported immense satisfaction.

As she drove to Adrienne's house to collect Mia, Harper reminded herself that she had a strong sense of who she was and what she wanted from life. Plus, unlike Stacy, she already had a child.

Whom she suddenly couldn't wait to hug.

ALL WEEK, PETER NOTICED whenever Harper arrived to drop off or collect her daughter at sports camp. Mostly, he gave her a friendly nod from a distance, despite the temptation to walk over and chat. He was here to work, and she had tasks to accomplish, as well.

The Fourth of July holiday fell midweek. Usually, he joined his parents for a barbecue, but this year they'd flown to Maryland to see his sister and meet Betty's new fiancé. Peter nearly asked Harper about her plans, except that would imply he wanted to be included. Instead, he volunteered to supervise a group of underprivileged children at an Independence Day festival.

On Friday, Peter missed seeing Harper. She must have been there, because Mia arrived and departed, but he got tied up with administrative matters. Thank goodness he had arranged to see her tomorrow.

Thank goodness? Peter's thoughts must have a mind of their own. He missed Angela too much to get involved with anyone else.

The memory of his wife reminded him that he'd been neglecting her rose garden. As a result, he spent Saturday morning deadheading flowers, fertilizing and spraying for black spot.

Although he planned to tramp around Harper's yard, he showered and changed into a fresh pair of jeans and a crisp, short-sleeved shirt. For good measure, he added a splash of aftershave lotion.

The address she'd provided was located a couple of miles across town, in a neighborhood of trim, one-story homes. He liked the clean lines of her house, while the bright flowers around the front steps welcomed him.

When the bell rang, footsteps pattered inside the house. Mia opened the door, her face shining with eagerness. "Mr. Gladstone!" She stepped back, tightening her grip on a black-and-white kitten, which responded by swiping her cheek with a closed paw. "This is Po."

"As in *Kung Fu Panda?*" he asked as he entered. The delicious scent of baking filled the air. Not just baking—chocolate.

"Yeah!" She shifted her grip on the wiggly animal. "Want to hold him?"

"Cats don't usually let strangers hold them," he observed.

"Okay." Swinging around, Mia bellowed, "Mom!" in a voice far too big for such a tiny sprite.

"I'll be right there," came the cheerful response. "I'm taking the brownies out of the oven."

He waited with Mia in the living room, which was solidly furnished with a dark brown sofa and a large entertainment center. Angela had relegated their TV to Peter's study, lining the front room with glass-front cabinets displaying decorative figurines and plates. Being surrounded by so much fragility made Peter feel as if he had to watch his step, but every couple compromised. He'd venture to guess that the large-screen TV had been more Sean's idea than Harper's.

She appeared with her short chestnut hair rumpled and her cheeks flushed from the heat of the oven. "Hey, Peter. Right on time. I appreciate this."

"Glad to help." He produced a pair of disposable cameras. "I had these left over from a science class and figured the guests could use them."

"Great idea!" Harper set them on the coffee table. "I suggested on the invitation that the kids bring cameras, but not everyone will. Now, while the brownies are cooling, let me show you the yard."

They cut through a large, modern kitchen and out via sliding glass doors to the patio. There, a slatted cover shaded a table, chairs and a glider. Beyond spread a lawn rimmed by bushes.

Mia released the kitten, which prowled across the lawn. The little girl followed, keeping a close eye on her baby.

"My brain's working overtime on decorations and stuff," Harper said. "I'm just not sure how to handle the bug hunt."

Peter made a circuit of the yard, checking for spiderwebs, anthills and other signs of creepy-crawlies. Afternoon wasn't the best time to look, since insects were more active in the mornings and evenings, but this was when the kids would be hunting.

As he pointed out activity, Harper took notes. "I have to fight my instinct to knock down that web," she said when they spotted a large one stretching from the rear fence to a nearby bush.

"It's huge!" Mia glanced protectively at Po, as if the kitten might wind up in the arachnid's snare.

This was the kind of teachable moment Peter relished. "That's an orb weaver web," he said. "I doubt it will be there tomorrow, let alone next week, but there might be a new one. Orb weavers consume their webs late in the day, rest for an hour or so and then spin a new one in the same area. You can see there isn't much detritus—old stuff like leaves stuck in it."

As Harper and her daughter peered intently at the web, Peter noted their resemblance, from their sturdy stance—legs apart, as if braced to run from a ferocious spider—to the mixture of fascination and revulsion in their green eyes. Would he see the same reactions in his own future child?

Peter tore his attention away to concentrate on Mia's next question, which was, "Are they poisonous?"

"Orb weavers do have venom," he confirmed. "That's

how they paralyze their prey. But they don't often bite people, and the venom isn't nearly as strong as a black widow's."

"All the same, I can't put the children at risk," Harper said.

"It's no greater a risk than getting dehydrated in the heat or being bonked by a soccer ball." Growing up intrigued by such critters, Peter had never worried about the danger. "You're lucky I'm not your kid. I used to freak out my mother by bringing home snakes."

"Ick! Ick!" Mia jumped around as if a real snake had appeared.

"Nonpoisonous ones." Peter chuckled at her antics. "But for the party, you should advise the kids not to touch anything."

"Like we would!" the little girl cried.

"Most bugs are harmless," he advised.

"Ick!" That seemed to be her favorite word.

"You wouldn't mind if a butterfly landed on you, would you?" When she shook her head, Peter went on. "Some creatures just need better public relations. However, I agree about not touching spiders. There are dangerous varieties in Southern California gardens and sheds, like black widows and brown recluses. You should never turn over rocks or poke around a garage without heavy gloves."

"What if an orb weaver did bite you?" Harper clearly hadn't lost track of their subject.

"You might experience localized pain." Such facts stuck in Peter's brain because he found biology fascinating. "You'd feel some numbness and swelling, possibly a blister. If there's nausea or dizziness, you should go to the emergency room, but usually the symptoms pass within twenty-four hours."

"Gee, that's reassuring," Harper drawled, and shut her

notebook. "Mia, you can help me tell the other kids what Mr. Gladstone said, but don't scare them unnecessarily."

"Can I scare them necessarily?" she asked.

"Arm them with the facts," Peter suggested. "That's what teaching is about. Giving people knowledge so they can draw rational conclusions."

As the three of them returned to the house, Harper said, "So—just for the sake of argument—you don't think it's your role to shape young minds? I heard a school board member say that was the purpose of education."

"Only to shape their minds in terms of being logical and informed," Peter told her. "Okay, I guess my moral values get involved, too, but I would never usurp the role of a parent. I'd hate if someone tried to indoctrinate my child in a way I disagreed with." He amended, "If I had a child."

Harper didn't appear to notice the wistful note in his voice. Or, if she did, she tactfully refrained from commenting.

Mia dashed ahead of them. Peter assumed she was chasing the kitten, which had slipped inside through the partly open glass door. When they entered, though, she reappeared with a squiggly green invitation.

Holding it out, she said, "Will you come to my party, Mr. Gladstone? There'll be cake and ice cream."

"Honey, Mr. Gladstone is doing us a favor today," Harper cautioned as she picked up a pizza cutter and sliced the brownies into squares. "Of course, you'd be more than welcome," she added.

To cover his hesitation, Peter read the details. The party was next Sunday afternoon, which didn't conflict with any of his plans. And it would be much more fun than weeding Angela's herb garden, which was what he ought to be doing. "I accept with pleasure."

On the kitchen table, Harper set out plates and glasses

of milk. Peter observed a few cookbooks wedged between canisters on the counter, and a spice rack filled with bottles. Otherwise, the kitchen was uncluttered, with simple, tan curtains—but then, this might be a rental.

Peter was still savoring his brownie when Mia finished wolfing down hers, drained her milk and jumped up. "Can I look for bugs? I won't touch them."

"Sure, go ahead," her mother said.

"You won't mind, Mr. Gladstone?"

Her politeness impressed him. "Actually, that's a great idea. And when we're away from sports camp, you can call me Peter."

"Okay. Thanks, Peter!"

The little girl raced out. Through the glass door, she and Po could be seen peering into the bushes. Peter wasn't sure which he liked most, the antics of the little ones or Harper's doting expression while observing them.

"You have a terrific little girl," Peter said. "She's quite intelligent."

"You've inspired her." She turned toward him.

"I live to inspire," he joked.

"Honestly, I think you do." Having quartered her brownie, Harper nibbled on a section. She didn't need to diet, but Peter had learned never to correct a woman about her personal regime. Even easygoing Angela had set him straight about that.

"How many people are coming to the party?" he asked.

"We invited ten kids." Harper reached to brush back her hair, and seemed disconcerted not to encounter any long strands. "Stacy and her fiancé are helping with the food. Adrienne's on the outdoor team. I'm not sure if any other parents will stay."

"No grandparents?" He assumed that his own parents would be involved in all important events for his future children. It wouldn't surprise him if his mother was already planning the baby's first Christmas.

"We're out of luck in the grandparent department." Harper stretched, and her long legs bumped his. "Sorry."

"No problem." Peter rather enjoyed the contact. "No grandparents at all?" It occurred to him that, while her profile indicated no known genetic problems, it had stated that neither of her parents was living.

"My dad died in a car crash when I was sixteen," she said. "My mom had a fatal stroke five years ago. She'd been a heavy smoker."

"That's too bad." How terrible to have lost even one parent, let alone both. "If you don't mind my asking, what about Sean's family?" Peter wasn't sure what prompted his curiosity, since Sean's background didn't affect Harper's role as an egg donor. He just wished Mia had at least one grandparent in her life.

Harper rolled her eyes. "After his parents divorced, his dad remarried and moved to Alaska. With him, it's out of sight, out of mind. I'm not complaining, though. He's never been difficult like Sean's mother."

"Difficult in what way?"

"Critical and disapproving, even when we were in high school, although Hedy didn't object to our marrying once we graduated from college," Harper said. "Then she moved back to her home state of Georgia with Sean's two sisters. She pushed for us to move there, too, and blamed me when we didn't. It was as much Sean's decision as mine."

"Surely she doesn't hold that against her granddaughter."

"I'll let you be the judge." Harper's mouth twisted. "One of my sisters-in-law has children a little older than Mia. Last Christmas, Hedy sent Mia their castoff clothes and a few used toys as her present."

"Were those expensive clothes and gently used toys?" Although most people expected new items for their kids, Peter sympathized with reusing special items, such as a classic dollhouse or favorite books.

"We're talking about jeans that were too small and stuffed animals with the fur worn off." Harper wrinkled her nose. "This week, for Mia's birthday, she sent a faded doll and a pair of old slippers."

That was ridiculous. "Do you suppose she has dementia?"

"It's hard to tell. She's always been self-centered and stingy." At her seat, Harper gathered their plates and glasses. "I don't believe in lavishing piles of gifts on children, but choosing with care, even if it's a pair of pretty socks, shows love."

"What did you tell Mia?"

"The truth," she responded. "That some people aren't generous or loving. And that having to deal with them helps us empathize with others who have even less than we do."

What a great response, Peter thought. "She must miss her dad."

"Sometimes, although his memory's starting to fade." Harper rose to clean up. "I try to keep him alive for her through videos and talking about things he used to say or do."

"She seems to be thriving." He wished all his campers were as cooperative and patient as Mia. Her friend Reggie, although basically a good kid, had thrown a couple of temper tantrums.

"It helps having you pitch in." Harper cast him a quick smile. "Your presence at the party will mean a lot."

"I'm sure I'll enjoy it as much as she will." When he

didn't have to deal with discipline or lesson plans, being around kids was fun.

After thanking her for the snack, Peter hit the road. Driving home, he wished these upbeat feelings could last. Instead, he had to face the downside of liking them so much.

There was no way he could raise her biological child or children without telling her. True, knowing where they came from and seeing Harper's positive traits in them would relieve Peter's concerns about using eggs from a stranger. And there might be advantages to having them meet their biological mother and half sister.

But the situation would be fraught with danger. Emotions were unpredictable. If he and Harper were to get involved and then break up, the consequences for the kids could be devastating.

Although she appeared the best match for him at Safe Harbor's egg bank, the director had assured Peter that he could also access the registries of other banks in the region. And that, he concluded reluctantly, was what he had to do.

Chapter Four

Steam from the outdoor whirlpool transformed the enclosure, with its mesh safety fence, into a secluded hideaway, an impression enhanced by the border of rosebushes and hibiscuses. Peter leaned back and let the heated swirl of water soothe his muscles.

"Worn-out from all that heavy-duty exercise?"

He cracked one eyelid in response to his father's sarcasm. Rod Gladstone was grinning, white teeth and silver hair a marked contrast to his tanned skin.

"Some of us try to actually move around and hit the ball when we play Ping-Pong," Peter retorted. "Which might explain why I beat you four-one."

"If I didn't have a bum knee…"

"I'd have beaten you four-one at tennis instead of Ping-Pong," Peter finished. "However, I'd be willing to adjust the score in deference to your great age and infirmity."

"Sixty-eight is not a great age. I can still do this." With the heel of his hand, Rod sent hot water spraying over Peter.

Spluttering, he was about to respond in kind when his mother's voice broke in. "Children, children." Widening her eyes with mock horror, Kerry Gladstone set down her tablet computer on the small glass table near the spa.

Peter refrained. "Grow up, Dad."

"Guess I'd better, considering I'm about to be a grand-father."

"Not *that* soon," Peter grumbled. His parents had re-turned yesterday from their trip, and while he'd been glad for their impromptu invitation to a late-Sunday-afternoon barbecue, he was in no mood to be pressured.

"Rod!" Kerry cast a longing eye at the computer, her favorite tool for her beloved genealogy research, but left it shut. "I thought we agreed our news could wait."

"What news?" Peter asked.

"She's right about waiting." Rod rose, dripped heav-ily onto his son and stepped from the pool. "That chicken should be done by now. I marinated it with a new recipe we got from Betty."

Peter had to admit, the scent of chicken grilling with garlic and oranges made it hard to concentrate. Still, he felt as if he'd missed a clue, or several. "Since when does my sister cook?" An ambitious lawyer, Betty worked hundred-hour weeks for a firm in Washington, D.C., commuting from her home in nearby Maryland. "What's up, guys?"

"It's hard to have a conversation on an empty stomach," Rod returned, drying off with an oversize towel.

A tendency to tease was *not* one of his father's more endearing traits, Peter thought as he hauled himself to dry land and grabbed his own towel. "Mom?" Kerry Gladstone had always been an easier mark.

As anticipated, she yielded. "Rod, it's not fair to keep him in suspense."

His father shrugged.

"Nothing's wrong, is it?" They'd already answered his questions about their trip—they liked Betty's fiancé, a fel-low attorney named Greg Southern, and the couple were planning a small wedding next month. Peter's invitation should be arriving shortly.

"Your sister's pregnant," Kerry said.

Peter caught his breath. Betty, having a baby? His single-minded sister had resisted the very idea of motherhood. "So, uh…" he managed to say.

"It was an accident, but a happy one now that she's had time to consider." Rod dropped his joking tone.

"She's due in January," Kerry added. "She plans to take three months' leave and then work on a reduced schedule."

"Which means sixty-hour weeks, right?" Peter knew his workaholic sister too well.

Kerry and Rod exchanged glances. There was more, he gathered. "And?" Peter pressed.

"It's a girl," his father said. "They haven't picked a name."

Peter pinned his gaze on his mother. "And?" he repeated.

She tucked the tablet into its case. "I can't bear for my granddaughter to grow up in day care. Besides, Betty will need our support." She stopped.

Rod blew out a long breath. "Moving to Maryland wasn't part of our retirement plans, but there's a lot of exciting stuff to do in the area. The National Archives alone could take years to explore."

They were doing *what?* A hundred thoughts collided in Peter's brain, sending up a wall of white noise.

Having dropped their bombshell, his parents went to finish preparing the meal. Although it was dinnertime, July sunlight bathed their backyard with its flagstone patio and outdoor kitchen. For years, they'd poured loving care into this comfortable home in the Orange County town of Yorba Linda, nesting for their retirement. Now they were leaving it?

More than that, they were leaving Peter. And his future children.

On automatic, he helped set the table and fetched potato salad and coleslaw from the refrigerator. As they ate, his parents filled him in on their plans to sell the house, with the goal of settling into a new home before the baby's birth.

I was counting on you. He didn't speak the words aloud, though. While his parents had more or less promised to help with his future family, Betty had an equal claim to their support. And she was pregnant, whereas he had no guarantees of what might happen.

The chicken might have been delicious, but Peter hardly noticed. He had to focus on saying the right things and hiding the fact that he felt blindsided.

What was he going to do?

Finally his parents fell silent. Glancing in front of him, Peter was surprised to see he'd eaten a slice of apple pie. All he had to show for it was the lingering taste of cinnamon.

"Well?" Kerry said.

"I don't think he heard the question," Rod murmured.

"What question?" Peter asked.

"We asked if you'd consider moving, too." Worry lines creased his mother's face. With her strawberry-blond hair and trim figure, she didn't usually look her sixty-seven years. Now, though, Peter registered how old she was becoming.

He expected to be there for his parents, just as they'd always been here for him. Wasn't it a son's duty to help his folks as they aged, assisting with medical and financial choices? But a pair of lawyers were better qualified to do that than he was.

"I can't." That was Peter's first reaction, and the more he thought about it, the less he could see any way around it. "It's not as if I can just pick up and land another job."

"It's not impossible," his father said. "They have schools in Maryland."

"It isn't that easy." Each state had its own requirements for a teaching credential. That might require taking classes, delaying his job prospects. Moreover, the situation would set back his quest to have children by at least a year. "I'd have to start all over with finding a fertility program and interviewing surrogates. And the delay...well, who knows?" While most thirty-one-year-old men might not be concerned about fertility, Peter faced extra obstacles.

His mother blinked hard. Hoping he hadn't made her cry, Peter reached across the table to cup her hand. She gave him a shaky smile. "We realize we dropped this on you like a ton of bricks."

"It's not as if we're moving tomorrow," his father put in. "And you wouldn't have to join us immediately, either."

"I promise to think about it." That was the best Peter could do.

After dinner, they discussed his mom's latest findings about the family history. Using historical records, she'd traced her ancestry back to some colorful characters, including a buccaneer who'd sailed with Sir Francis Drake. Now she was working on his father's origins.

All the while, Peter's brain hummed with the startling news about his parents. He could tell it lingered in their minds, too, although they avoided the topic until he was ready to leave.

"It's not as if we'll be living in another country," Kerry said as she embraced him.

"Or on another planet, although that *would* be interesting," his father added.

"I'll email Betty my congratulations." Except for birthdays and major holidays, Peter had fallen into the habit of relying on his parents for updates about his older sister. He missed their closeness when they were younger.

That had ended when Betty entered high school. From freshman year forward, she'd focused on earning top grades, racking up extracurricular honors and aiming for a top school. She'd made it into Yale and later Harvard Law, while he'd attended the University of California's campus in Riverside, less than an hour's drive from home.

Her career sizzled, and her income must be quadruple his. But Peter had a job he loved and no regrets.

He'd like to live near her and certainly near his parents, he conceded as he drove back to Safe Harbor. And having a cousin nearby should be good for his kids.

If he ever had any.

His chest tightened. He didn't mean to be negative. All things were possible these days, but the idea of relocating threw a monkey wrench into his plans.

Arriving at his cottage, Peter wondered how he could leave the house he'd shared with Angela. She'd loved this place. He'd contributed personal touches, as well, transforming the workshop behind the garage into a gym. As for the fertility program, while he assumed the D.C. area had plenty of medical facilities, he'd made an emotional connection here, with his doctor and with the other personnel.

Not to mention Harper.

An image of her popped into his mind—her athletic stride, her funny way of trying to stroke her long hair and then remembering that she'd cut it, her tenderness with her daughter.

Thinking of Mia reminded him of next weekend's party. In the future nursery, Peter examined the contents of the bookshelf. Because he wrote a blog reviewing biology-related books for students, publishers sent him their latest offerings, including some for younger readers. As a result, he had a number of like-new children's books on insects, reptiles and animals.

Peter flipped through several picture books about bugs for preschoolers and a couple of illustrated volumes for slightly older readers. If he were to write such a story, it would feature more in-depth information and photographs rather than drawings.

The idea of writing about biology for children had occurred to him before, only to be abandoned because he never found the right angle. In this crowded field, Peter knew, a book required a unique angle and a distinctive look to make it stand out.

He selected the best of the batch for Mia. It had been fun yesterday, touring Harper's yard and explaining about spiders. He could still see Mia scrunching her little face and asking, "Can I scare them necessarily?"

Longing swept through Peter, to have a child like her. A small, precious person to hold, to nurture, to stretch out his arms to as she took those first steps. Waiting another year or more, taking a chance with a different donor...but then, even if he stayed in California, he'd already decided against raising a youngster near her biological mother, especially one who was a friend.

Abruptly, a possibility occurred to Peter. He went cold and then hot, as if he were coming down with something.

To clear his head, he retreated to the backyard. Stars glittered in the summer sky, in defiance of the light pollution from houses and streetlamps. The scents of Angela's herbs—mint and lemon balm—soothed his spirit. Yet when he tried to picture her, the face he saw belonged to Harper.

If he moved out of state, he'd never see her again. While that troubled him, he wasn't ready for a serious relationship, anyway.

He could proceed with the surrogate he'd chosen, use Harper's eggs and have a child or children like Mia. In Maryland, the little one would grow up surrounded by family, and far from his or her biological mother.

Peter hated the idea of keeping his plan a secret from Harper. Yet if they shared the experience of a pregnancy, if she ever held a baby that belonged to them both, he'd be inviting the type of legal and emotional tangle that he was determined to avoid.

Sitting on a wrought-iron bench beside the path, he took out his phone and brought up the egg donor site. Harper's statement said she was eager to help others form a family, that she was willing to meet the recipients or not. So, what was the difference whether the recipient was someone she knew?

Especially if he planned to leave.

While the deception bothered Peter, other considerations overrode that. As for moving, the idea was growing on him. He wasn't nearly as in love with this house as his wife had been, and he had a year to resolve the job situation.

On the phone, he did some quick research. It appeared that Maryland accepted California teacher certifications. While he might have to take a few tests, that shouldn't present a major obstacle.

Contrary to what he'd first thought, his parents hadn't knocked a hole in his plans. Instead, they'd handed him a solution to his dilemma.

On Friday morning, Harper felt her phone vibrate as she finished prepping Una for an ultrasound. Stepping into the hallway, she saw that the call came from Melissa Everhart, who coordinated the egg donor and IVF programs under Jan Garcia's direction.

Had someone chosen Harper? Despite the quickening of her pulse, she was too busy to return the call now. She'd only checked in case Mia was having a problem at sports camp.

The ultrasound technician, Zora Raditch, pushed her equipment cart past Harper and into the examining room. The normally vivacious woman in her late twenties had dark circles under her eyes. As everyone knew, she was suffering through a painful divorce from her cheating husband.

Harper gave her a sympathetic nod. She'd have offered more support, except that Zora had cheated *with* her louse of a husband several years ago while he was married to Stacy. If nothing else, that should have provided a strong clue to his character.

At the nurses' station, Harper made sure no last-minute patients had been squeezed into the schedule before lunch. No one had, which left her free to return to the ultrasound.

She'd reached the room when Stacy hurried alongside, no doubt having just finished assisting at a surgery. "Jim's out of town," she explained breathlessly. That was Una's husband, a long-distance truck driver. "Una asked me to be here."

"No problem," said Nora Franco, appearing behind them. With a smile, the obstetrician added, "I love the way you two have bonded."

"I wonder if my triplets can sense when they're in the same room as their half siblings," Stacy mused as she preceded them inside.

Una, reclining on an examining table as Zora readied her equipment, beamed at them. "You bet they can!"

Zora and Stacy exchanged quick nods of acknowledgment. Working at the same complex had been awkward for the two women, but recently they'd reached a sort of truce.

Stacy went to hold Una's hand. The technician spread gel on the patient's abdomen and gently applied the paddle-shaped sensor device. On the monitor, black and white eddies yielded to the curling shapes of two babies.

Instinctively, Harper touched her own flat stomach, recalling when she'd undergone this experience with Mia. What a miracle, to see her little girl for the first time. Sean had practically levitated off the floor.

She got an extra squiggle of exhilaration as she recalled the phone message awaiting her response. Maybe she'd been chosen. In a few months, she might be watching her own genetic baby or babies inside the surrogate.

On the screen, the little ones' hands met over their hearts. As one of the pair shifted toward the other, Una said, "It almost looks like they're playing."

"They might be," Nora said. "We now know that twins do interact in the womb."

"Interact how?" Stacy asked.

"Researchers taped ultrasound images of twins and studied the recordings," the doctor explained. "It became clear that the fetuses were deliberately stroking each other."

"So when a mother pats her tummy and gets a bump in return, that's intentional?" Harper had loved when that happened with Mia.

"Apparently so." Nora smiled. "Of course, we moms have always suspected as much, haven't we?"

Heads nodded and warm fellowship filled the room. Except for Zora, Harper noted; the ultrasound tech stayed focused on her work, lips pressed tightly together. Unlike the other women, she had no children.

"Can you tell the gender?" Una asked.

"It's kind of early." The technician shot a questioning look at the doctor. "It may be another month before we can tell."

"It depends on the babies," Nora said. "If they want to show us by moving into the right positions, we can make a good guess."

At Una's urging, the paddle moved across her abdomen, pressing more firmly. As the babies wiggled, the tech said, "There! That might be a boy."

"He appears to have the right equipment," Nora observed.

"How cute!" Una pumped the air. "Now, is he having a brother or a sister?"

After a few more minutes, the doctor said, "There she goes! Well, I think it's a she. Don't hold me to that."

"A boy and a girl." Una grinned. "Just what I want. But I'd be happy with two of a kind."

Now that she'd learned the news, Harper slipped out of the room. They didn't need her there, and she was missing her lunch break.

More important, she had a phone call to return.

Chapter Five

The other staffers must have gone out for lunch, Harper noted as she entered the break room. Grateful for the privacy, she returned Melissa's call.

"Good news!" the coordinator said after greeting her. "You've been selected as a donor."

The room blurred, and Harper leaned against the wall for support. Hard to believe this was really happening. Those two little boys wouldn't remain a fantasy much longer.

"Do they want to meet me?" she asked.

"He said that isn't necessary." In the background, the clink of dishes indicated Melissa was in the hospital cafeteria. "Hold on. I don't want anyone overhearing our conversation."

He? Harper wondered while she waited for the coordinator to move to a more private place. A single dad? Although Harper had indicated on the form that she was willing to work with a single parent, she'd been picturing a couple, or possibly a single mom.

After a moment, Melissa spoke again. "He's selected a surrogate and she's good to go this month."

A surrogate. So she wouldn't be dealing with a happy, loving mom like Una. But obviously not, with a single father involved.

Well, so what? Harper trusted the program, and fate. Someone had chosen her to be the mother of his child. That was what counted.

"We can start coordinating your cycles right away if that's all right," Melissa continued.

Right away? Something so momentous seemed like it ought to take longer. Still, Harper saw no reason to delay.

During the first part of the donation process, the egg donor's and the recipient's menstrual cycles had to be synchronized through the use of birth control pills. That ensured that the mom or, in this case, the surrogate would be physically ready to receive the eggs when they were mature. It was a delicate, intimate process that Harper had looked forward to sharing with the other woman.

"Will I be meeting the surrogate?" she asked.

"I'm afraid not," Melissa replied gently. "I realize that's a letdown, after you've psyched yourself up, but I did tell you that your experience might differ from Stacy's."

Harper struggled to adjust to the notion that she'd be undergoing this process alone, except for the staff's support. After three to six weeks of preparation, her eggs—hopefully a dozen or more—would be harvested. There'd be no mom or dad to witness the thrilling event. After the eggs were fertilized, healthy embryos would be implanted in the surrogate.

The process loomed as cold and impersonal, not what Harper had imagined. But while she had the right to change her mind, that didn't seem fair. She'd agreed to this. Also, how would she explain a change of heart to Mia, after all the buildup about giving the gift of life to a family?

Onto her mental landscape flashed an image of two little boys romping in a field, giggling and playing catch with a blurry figure. *Their father.*

This wasn't about Harper. It was about her sons. No, *his* sons.

"I take it the father has been carefully screened?" Despite knowing the answer, she craved reassurance.

"He's a widower," Melissa told her. "He works with children professionally. That's all I can reveal, but we've run a background check and a psychological profile, as with all our parents, and he'll make a wonderful dad."

A widower who worked with children. For some reason, Peter came to mind. But he'd never mentioned trying to have kids and, besides, that description must fit a lot of men.

He was in her thoughts because she'd seen him this morning when she dropped off her daughter. Harper could have sworn Peter's expression had brightened when he greeted her, although that might be wishful thinking.

In that case, what was she wishing for?

She returned her attention to the phone. "When do we start?"

"Dr. Sargent can see you this afternoon, if Dr. Franco will spare you for a little while." Obstetrician Zack Sargent, husband of program director Jan Garcia, would be supervising Harper's care and harvesting the eggs.

She swallowed a lump in her throat. *No one promised you'd be able to bond with the children's parents.*

Concentrating on the afternoon's schedule, she did some quick calculations. Nora's partner, Dr. Paige Brennan, took off Friday afternoons to spend with her five-month-old daughter. Paige's nurse, Keely Randolph, stayed a few hours afterward to order supplies and catch up on other tasks. She might be willing to fill in for Harper. "I'll see if I can duck out. Can I call you right back?"

"Absolutely," Melissa assured her.

A few minutes later, Harper had coordinated the plans.

After a bite of her sandwich, she was on her way to Dr. Sargent's office, on the same floor as Nora's.

BETWEEN WORKING AND moving ahead with his plans, Peter's week flew by. He designated Harper as the egg donor, signed legal papers and transferred into his checking account the money to pay out in the coming month.

The wheels were turning. If all went well, in less than a year, he'd become a father. On Saturday night, sitting in his living room surrounded by Angela's cabinets and curios, Peter found himself talking to her.

"We were supposed to go on this journey together." He addressed an angel figurine that reminded him of his wife. About seven inches high with wings ornamented by flower designs, the girl clutched an armful of daisies to her chest. "You told me to use your life insurance to have children, so you're part of this, too. I'm not leaving you behind, honey. I will never do that."

He didn't care if someone else might consider him foolish. He wanted to reassure Angela, and himself, that they were in this together.

In the quiet room, he listened to the hum of electricity and the distant murmur of cars. The figurine's expression remained serene.

"If it's a little girl, I'll name her after you," he promised. "If it's a boy, well, all bets are off." Her father's name had been Cecil, and Peter was not going to burden his son with that.

Something nagged at the back of his mind. It had to do with Harper.

Although he'd made a rational decision not to reveal his involvement, Peter wasn't entirely satisfied with that. He had no desire to take advantage of her.

On the other hand, as much as he valued Harper's contribution and as much as he liked and respected her, this wasn't their journey as a couple. Each of them had a separate path in life.

Perhaps it would be a mistake to attend her daughter's party tomorrow. He didn't mean to give the impression that he was an intimate part of their world. But how could he disappoint Mia? On Friday afternoon, she'd been jumping up and down with excitement, reminding him to arrive at two o'clock.

Cutting them off would be cruel. It might also raise questions in Harper's mind. Peter knew he ran a risk of having her discover the truth, since she worked next door to the hospital.

He'd attend tomorrow. But after that, Peter needed to ease out of her life. It was the best course for everyone.

HARPER DIDN'T RUSH TO spread the news to her friends. She'd rather not explain over the phone or by email that she'd been selected by a single dad, that he didn't want to meet her and that she was beginning the process already. Better to wait and tell them in person.

On Saturday, she'd been too busy preparing for the party to see anyone. Now, on Sunday, she felt a twist of bittersweet longing as she welcomed Stacy and Cole, who'd come early to help.

Two days ago, she'd enjoyed seeing Stacy and Una's shared happiness at the ultrasound. Now she struggled to absorb her own very different reality.

You have to tell her. And she would. Later.

On Friday, after a checkup to confirm she remained in good health, Zack Sargent had provided her with the birth control pills to start synchronizing her cycle and the surrogate's. Although Harper expected to see him today when he and Jan dropped off their daughters, they certainly wouldn't be discussing her medical treatment.

For now, she concentrated on organizing the refreshments. Attempting to help, Mia chattered and jumped about until she knocked over a stack of plastic cups.

"I'm sorry, Mommy." She scooped them up.

"No harm done."

It was a relief when Adrienne arrived with Reggie and the children exploded out the door. He and Mia chased each other around the patio, batting at the green balloons and streamers that were supposed to resemble vines. They put on antenna headbands Harper had made and hopped about shaking the black pipe cleaners and white pompoms. Po retreated, meowing in distress, until Harper carted him to the safety of the laundry room.

She emerged to see Adrienne, her long blond hair clipped back, pacing off the length of a competition course in the backyard. She'd agreed to organize outdoor games to intersperse with the bug hunt.

Harper went outside to welcome her friend. "I can't tell you how much I appreciate this."

"As if you didn't help me whenever I need it." Adrienne displayed a bag filled with plastic bugs. "I brought these as prizes. Everybody can take home a handful."

"Those are darling." Taking a closer look, Harper couldn't help murmuring, "And creepy, too."

"Vicki and I used to sneak toy spiders into each other's beds." As always at the mention of her late sister, a shadow crossed Adrienne's face. "Sometimes months would go by. Just when I'd almost forgotten them, she'd scare the heck out of me. Or I'd do it to her. It was fun."

"I miss her, too." Harper and Stacy had been close to Vicki since junior high, sharing youthful crushes, playing computer games and helping one another with homework.

When Harper's father died, it was Vicki and Stacy who'd stood by her, just as much as Sean.

When Vicki developed bipolar disorder, they'd rallied around her. But as she reached her twenties, her condition had deteriorated, especially after Reggie was born. Abandoned by the little boy's father, Vicki had begun abusing alcohol.

Last New Year's Eve, their friend had gone out drinking and crashed her car into a telephone pole. She'd died at the scene. It was lucky that Adrienne had already moved into the family's home and taken on much of the responsibility for Reggie.

The doorbell rang, summoning Harper into the house. It was seven-year-old Fiona Denny with her stepmother, Patty. With barely a "Hi, Harper," the little girl raced outside to join Mia and Reggie.

"She loves anything to do with science, just like her dad," Patty said. An embryologist, Alec Denny was director of laboratories for the fertility program. "Watch out or she'll start dissecting insects with a kitchen knife."

"She does that?" Harper asked.

"Not yet, but we've had to stitch all her stuffed animals back together." Patty shook her head. "Her dad thinks her ready to start doing experiments for real. I'm glad he's willing to help. My reaction to bugs is to step on them."

Harper remembered what Peter had said. "You're lucky she doesn't bring home snakes."

"Oh, I'd shoot those." A former police officer, Patty now worked as a private detective.

"You still carry a gun?" Harper had never seen her armed.

"No, but I practice at the gun range." Patty spotted a family approaching the open door. "Oh, hey, folks!"

Dr. Zack Sargent and his wife, Jan Garcia, had brought

their daughters, Kimmie and Berry. When she invited them to the party, Harper hadn't imagined that she'd be working with Zack so soon. But naturally they kept private and work lives separate.

There was no time to talk, with more children showing up. While Stacy and Cole were mixing the punch and setting out snacks, Harper distributed antenna headbands and magnifying lenses.

Gifts piled up on a side table. Outside, kids ran laughing and giggling under Adrienne and Patty's supervision. Declining their offer of help, she sent Zack and Jan to enjoy a rare child-free day. The parents of the other kids, Mia's school friends, didn't stick around, which was fine with Harper.

Where was Peter? It was nearly two-thirty, and no sign of him yet.

Hesitant to launch the bug hunt without him, Harper suggested Adrienne start the grasshopper jumping contest. Each child leaped in turn, with Patty marking the spot. The goal was to beat their own best distance. Those who succeeded could pick a plastic creepy-crawly from the bag.

With matters well in hand, Harper headed for the kitchen. Stacy and Cole appeared to be squabbling over the birthday cake. When they saw her, a guilty expression flashed over Cole's face.

"What's wrong?" Harper asked.

Stacy pointed at the frosted carrot cake, baked in a flat sheet. Cole had methodically traced a grid pattern over the surface—preparing to cut it into squares—and messed up the words *Happy Seventh Birthday, Mia.*

"I forgot about the candle thing," the surgeon said.

"How could you do that?" his fiancée scolded. "The kids haven't even seen it yet."

"My mother wasn't the birthday party type," Cole reminded her.

"No harm done." Harper thought fast. "We'll tell the kids you prepared it for surgery. A lot of them have parents in the medical field. They'll understand."

"Brilliant," Stacy said.

"This way they can eat sooner, too," her husband observed.

Kimmie Sargent wandered inside. "I need to go to the bathroom." When Harper pointed her in the right direction, she hurried off.

Stacy watched her with a motherly expression. "I can't wait to find out if we're having a little girl. I mean, out of three, the odds are pretty good, wouldn't you say?"

"It isn't hard to calculate," Cole told her. "Each child has a one-in-two chance of being a girl or a boy. You multiply that—"

His wife raised her hands. "It isn't all probabilities. Harper's certain she's got two little boys waiting to be born."

Cole merely looked confused.

"I hope someone picks you soon," Stacy said.

It was the perfect opening, so Harper jumped in. "As a matter of fact, I found out yesterday that I've been chosen."

"Fantastic!"

She summarized the events: Melissa's phone call, the revelation about a single dad and her decision to proceed.

Stacy listened wide-eyed. Cole's expression was detached, as if he'd shifted into physician mode. Second nature for him, Harper supposed.

"I'm going to be a mom, but I won't be part of the pregnancy or the birth," she concluded wistfully.

"You must be disappointed," Stacy said.

"As an egg donor, this is what I signed up for. Still, I'm

sorry I can't be more involved. I'll never even know if it's a girl or a boy. Or if there's more than one."

From the living room doorway came a rustling sound. Startled, Harper turned to see Peter, a wrapped gift in one hand, a pie in the other and a furrow between his eyebrows. How much had he heard?

"I didn't mean to intrude." He stepped aside to let Kimmie dodge past. Out she went via the patio slider. "That little girl let me in."

Harper's cheeks flamed. What was the last thing she'd said? If he'd learned that she was an egg donor, what did he think of it?

"I'm sorry I'm late," Peter added. "My parents dropped by unexpectedly. They had some information about my sister's upcoming wedding and they brought me a pie. I can't eat it all myself, so please accept this as a peace offering."

"No apology necessary." As Harper transferred the pie to the counter, the aroma of apples and cinnamon teased her senses. "Cole's happy to exercise his surgical skills on any and all desserts. Peter, I'd like you to meet my friends Cole and Stacy."

When the men shook hands, she saw a glint of recognition pass between them. If Peter was Cole's patient, it was none of her business, she thought. Still, why not just acknowledge that they knew each other?

"Gifts go on that table, I see." As Peter squared his shoulders, it drew Harper's attention to the slogan on his navy T-shirt: When Life Gives You Mold, Make Penicillin. How appropriate for a biologist.

"I think the grasshopper games are winding down," she said. "Come on out and I'll introduce you to everyone."

She resolved not to worry about what he might have heard. She and Peter were friends, nothing more. If the relationship developed later, there'd be plenty of time to discuss her decision to donate. As a scientist, surely he'd understand.

And if not, too bad. Harper wasn't living her life subject to a man's approval.

Chapter Six

That had been uncomfortable, Peter reflected—accidentally eavesdropping on Harper, and then shaking hands with Cole as if they were strangers. Neither he nor his doctor had figured out a better way to react on the spur of the moment.

That, however, was unimportant compared to the insight he'd gained into Harper's feelings. He was sorry she felt let down about the donation process. Peter had to admit that, while he'd given much thought to how she might relate to any future children, he hadn't realized she looked forward to being involved with the pregnancy.

Although it was minor by comparison, he hadn't meant to disappoint her by arriving late, either, but his parents had put in an unexpected appearance. They'd tried to call first, but Peter had accidentally left his phone off. Unable to reach him, Rod and Kerry had taken the chance of dropping by on their way to join friends for a barbecue.

They'd only meant to leave the pie, one of several his mother had baked that morning, but then they'd asked about the latest developments in his quest for fatherhood. Before he knew it, half an hour had passed.

Now, after giving Mia and Reggie a hug, he gathered the children for the hunt. They responded with enthusiasm when he explained that they were all scientists today—

that they'd be observing insect and spider activity, taking pictures and jotting notes on pads that he'd brought in his knapsack.

"When you get home, you can write about what you've seen, then combine your comments with your photos on pages so they look like books." That idea had struck him this morning, and he'd spent an hour researching and printing directions on how to lay out the pages so they could be printed, folded and stapled to give to parents and grandparents. This would reinforce their writing skills as well as encourage them to do more research on their computers. "I'll give you each an instruction sheet to take home. It'll be a fun project. I'm sure your parents will be glad to help you."

"We can make our own little books!" Mia cried.

"Exactly." The comment reminded Peter of his idea to write a children's book. But while it was easy to visualize the type of photos he'd like to include, he lacked the patience and the artistic eye to capture them. Speaking of photos… "Okay, who brought cameras and who needs one?"

"Mommy gave me one for my birthday." Mia waved a small camera.

Other children showed theirs or accepted the disposable ones Peter offered. With the aid of Harper's outdoor team—Reggie's aunt Adrienne, whom he'd met at sports camp, and a sturdy woman named Patty—he set to work.

Hard as he tried to put Harper's disappointment out of his mind, though, her words lingered. *I'll never even know if it's a girl or a boy.*

Occasionally, Peter sneaked a glance at Harper. If she was unhappy, you'd never guess it from the way she kept up with the kids. Her face alight, she teased the youngsters out of their squeamishness and assisted them with framing their shots.

"Don't use flash," she cautioned Reggie. "There's plenty of daylight, plus digital cameras have great resolution."

"What's that?" he asked.

"It means they're sensitive. They pick up all the details, even in dim light. Personally, I'd rather not have a flash on my camera at all."

"Where's your camera?" He indicated her empty hands.

"I left it inside, but I was out here this morning before the sun broke through the clouds," Harper said. "That's the best time to find bugs. The light is softer, too."

"I'll bet you took some great shots." Peter was impressed, and curious.

She swung toward him. "I'd be happy to show you, if you can stay a few minutes extra."

"Certainly." Although that would be risking drawing closer to Harper, seeing her photos would be fun. Surely he could handle a simple friendship based on shared interests.

For good measure, though, and to avoid giving anyone the impression that they were a couple, Peter did his best to keep his distance during the party. That wasn't difficult, since there was always a child to console over a tumble or a camera lens to clean after it fell in the dirt. Then Reggie and Mia got into a squabble over who had spotted a butterfly first, and he helped Adrienne separate them while Harper went to set out tuna, chicken and cheese sandwiches.

They were delicious, Peter discovered when he had a chance to eat. He liked the vegetables and dip, as well. "And there's health food for dessert," commented the woman standing next to him on the patio. Patty, that was her name.

"I beg your pardon?" Peter regarded the cake, which

looked so sweet his teeth ached. "Just because it's called carrot cake, that doesn't make it good for you."

"Sure it is," Patty responded, blithely indifferent to a few leaves clinging to her short blond hair. "If a tiny piece of vegetable falls into the mix or somebody eats a banana and breathes on it, it's health food."

Harper certainly had interesting friends, Peter thought as they watched Mia blow out her seven candles. The children crowded around eagerly for their perfectly square slices, although a few chose apple pie instead. Peter decided to skip dessert. Patty took a slice of each—to make up for him, she declared.

"I take it you aren't in the health care field," he said.

"That's my husband's department," she returned cheerily.

"He's a doctor?"

"Embryologist. Alec Denny."

"I've heard of him." The name Alec Denny, Ph.D., appeared on the roster of fertility program specialists. This woman's husband might even be the one who would inject Peter's sperm into the eggs. Safe Harbor was a small world.

And I'm likely to get caught if I'm not careful.

Finally the gifts had been opened, the punch bowl emptied and Peter's instruction sheets distributed. Parents arrived to claim their kids, while Harper's friends removed trash, stowed food and cleaned the kitchen. The only remaining traces of the party were a few surviving clusters of balloons and the vinelike streamers draping the patio.

Two little girls—Kimmie, who'd let Peter in at the door, and her stepsister, Berry—remained to play with Mia and her kitten. Their parents had phoned to say they'd bought new patio furniture on their shopping trip, and they'd be along as soon as they finalized arrangements.

"Actually, I'm glad," Harper told Peter as she set up

her laptop on the kitchen table. "Having the girls here will keep Mia occupied. Otherwise she'd be bouncing off the ceiling."

"After all that exercise?" He stretched, feeling the effects of the afternoon's intense activity. "At camp, the kids do wear out eventually."

"That must be a relief." Harper activated her photo editing program. "But at this age, I'm sure they get a second wind. Unlike high school students."

"What makes you say that?" Peter rested his elbows on the table.

"If I remember correctly, teenagers mostly want to sleep all day," she responded.

"A certain percentage of kids are kinetic—they learn best in motion." It required all Peter's patience and creativity to manage those students. "I fantasize about conducting classes on the athletic field. I'd be tempted to haul trampolines into the classroom if it wasn't for the liability."

"Spoken like a coach."

"True." He grinned at her accuracy.

"You enjoy athletics, don't you?"

"As a sideline." Sports camp presented a welcome change, for a few months. "I find teaching science more satisfying, though."

From the hallway came a burst of giggles. "Sounds like they're having fun. Kimmie and Berry are sweet kids."

"And your daughter's a charmer," Peter said.

It struck him that now would be a perfect time to mention that he was the dad who'd chosen her. He could allay her disappointment and invite her to…what? Become best buddies with his surrogate, Vanessa? And how would that change her relationship with him?

It went against Peter's nature to blurt such an important revelation without considering the consequences. He had to weigh the possibility that he might regret doing so.

Might regret it for the rest of his life, if she became too emotionally involved.

His attention shifted to the screen displaying row after row of pictures. Harper clicked on a stunning image of dewdrops shimmering like silver beads on a spiderweb. Close up, the wheel-spoke design of supporting threads and laddered rows achieved an astonishing symmetry.

"That's a remarkable shot," Peter said.

"I went out several mornings in a row before I spotted it." Harper switched to another photo, in different light, showing a similar web. "They're fascinating."

"It's hard to believe that's spun from a single continuous filament," Peter said.

"Here's one with the spider at work." She switched to a picture of a half-finished web, its eight-legged creator busily plying its thread.

As she leaned forward, the residual aroma of sun-warmed skin teased his senses. Despite his appreciation for the artistry of both spider and photograph, Peter had trouble concentrating on the picture. Instead, he observed how honey-colored strands added richness to Harper's chestnut hair, and how satiny her skin looked at close range.

Peter cleared his throat. "Your work shows a real gift. Ever think about doing that professionally?"

"I have to be realistic." Harper sat back. "Trying to earn a living at art photography is a good way to go broke. Oh, look at this one." On the laptop, she brought up a yellow-and-black butterfly on a red flower.

"That's brilliant." Peter recognized the coloring. "It's a dogface butterfly, the California state insect."

"We have a state insect?" Harper's mouth quirked. "Do we have a state spider, too?"

"Probably." If he knew what it was, though, it had slipped his mind. He found it hard to concentrate when the green of her blouse intensified the color of her eyes.

"Snakes? Rabbits?" Harper asked.

"I'm sorry?"

"Do we have a state bunny?" she prompted.

Somehow Peter dredged up a coherent response. "Not officially, but there is a domestic California rabbit that was bred here. It has big fat ears and it's mostly white except for dark feet, nose and tail."

"The stuff you know!"

And the stuff I can't help seeing. Such as that, from this angle, Harper's top clung to the inviting curve of her breasts.

He had no business lusting after her. It felt disloyal to Angela. Yet, for a startling moment, he almost resented his late wife.

To change the subject, he broached a topic he'd been toying with. "While I was picking out a book for Mia about insects, it occurred to me that I'd like to write one of my own someday. I'd use photos instead of illustrations, and go into the biology with more depth."

"What a great idea." Harper studied him admiringly. "I'll bet you'd have a blast."

"I *would* enjoy doing that." Despite the risks inherent in spending time with her, this presented an irresistible opportunity. "Would you be interested in collaborating?"

She paused with her fingers above the keyboard. "You mean, take the pictures for you?"

"You've already made a good start."

Her gaze swept the screen. "I guess I have, haven't I?"

Now that they were discussing it, Peter considered the practical side. "I have no idea how we'd find a publisher, or whether we'd earn any money. If we did, we'd split it."

"I hear a lot of people are publishing on the web." The fringe of lashes around her eyes seemed darker at close range, Peter noted irrelevantly. "As you say, it probably wouldn't pay much, but having my name on a book would give me a professional credit that could lead to occasional photography jobs. It might boost your reputation as a teacher, too."

They'd be working closely together—very closely. He'd better make sure there was no misunderstanding. "We'd have to finish it in a few months, before I move East."

The room became very quiet. The only noises were the refrigerator's hum and, from deep within the house, girlish chatter. It sounded like Mia and her friends were playing a game.

"You're…moving?" The question seemed to stick in Harper's throat.

Peter nodded.

Her mouth formed the word, "When?"

Although a lump had formed in his throat, as well, Peter pushed out the words, "Next summer. After school finishes."

"Oh," Harper said. "I didn't realize."

"It's a recent decision." But a good one. Today, Peter had planned to ease out of Harper's sphere, and instead he was carving out a larger role for himself. The deadline for his departure would make it easier to set boundaries. "My sister's having a baby. Since my parents decided to live close to her, I'm going, too."

"Where?" She kept her gaze trained on the screen.

"Maryland, in a suburb of D.C." Speaking about his plans gave them a kind of solidity. Until now, Peter hadn't confirmed the move to his parents, other than to mention he was considering it.

"The other side of the country."

"So it is." Having dropped that bombshell, Peter hoped he hadn't discouraged her from their project. "When's a good time for us to have a planning session?"

"For?"

"The book."

"Oh, right." She checked a calendar on the computer. "Mia has a ceramics workshop next Saturday. She's been dying to play around with clay, which gives me a free day."

"I'm free, too. How's 10:00 a.m.?"

She was entering it into her calendar when the doorbell rang. The Sargents had returned.

Peter said his farewells, accepted the remaining half of the pie at Harper's insistence and departed. All the while, his body reverberated with an awareness of her—the touch of their hands as he accepted the pie plate, the sweetly sad curve of her lips as she murmured goodbye.

Perhaps joining forces on this book was a mistake. But Harper's photos had provided the special quality he'd been searching for. This might be his only chance to put his ideas into action.

Peter could steer this course smoothly. He wasn't some hormonal adolescent with a crush.

And so, when he arrived home, he set to researching children's books currently published on backyard biology, both in his collection and online. The more he studied what was available, the more he became convinced that his— his and Harper's—would be special.

PULLING DOWN THE CREPE paper streamers after the Sargents left, Harper tried to calm her ricocheting emotions. Sitting with Peter, aware of the strength of his body next to hers, she'd felt something beyond physical attraction. A bond, a shared eagerness and a sense of vistas opening before her.

Not only did the prospect of putting her photos to use

thrill her, but—at first—she'd imagined that working closely with him would give their friendship a chance to develop naturally. None of those awkward are-we-dating-yet? issues. Instead, they'd have an opportunity to discover if they meshed on more than a casual basis.

Moreover, unlike with Sean, she wouldn't have to set aside her passion for photography. Quite the opposite: Peter inspired her with fresh ideas.

Being around him sparked her intellectually and awakened a longing to be held and caressed. Harper had underestimated how much she craved that kind of connection.

But he was moving away. Several thousand miles away. Best to put him out of her mind.

With a sigh, Harper shoved the last of her decorations into the trash can. The party had been a hit, leaving Mia happy to snuggle up with Po for a rare nap before dinner.

Harper was free to spend her time as she chose: sorting through her photos, deleting the weaker shots and touching up the stronger ones. But after a few minutes, she discovered that she needed to rest. Her breasts felt sore, a side effect of the birth control pills. Ironic that she and the surrogate were taking pills developed to prevent conception as the first stage in the fertility process.

Thinking about the babies-to-be lightened her mood. She was involved in a project far more important than a children's book.

She'd rather not tell Peter what she was doing, Harper decided. He'd be gone soon, and this was too precious to share with someone who was only passing through her life. If he'd overheard any of her conversation with Stacy and Cole, he'd given no indication, and surely had the discretion not to bring it up.

She'd keep him safely compartmentalized. With so much going on, that shouldn't be difficult.

Chapter Seven

By midweek, Harper still felt sore, plus she'd gained a few pounds, another side effect of the pills. Eating cake at the party hadn't helped, she conceded.

Another week to go. According to Zack, that would coordinate her cycle and the surrogate's. Then she'd have to self-administer hormone shots daily for a week, to stop the normal functioning of her ovaries. It all seemed so contradictory, when the point was to produce eggs, but this was how the system worked.

On Wednesday morning, a couple of Nora's appointments canceled, leaving both her and Harper with a long lunch break. By contrast, Dr. Paige Brennan had to work in a couple of patients.

"Do you want me to prep the next one?" Harper asked Keely, aware that she owed the other nurse a favor.

Without speaking, her coworker handed her a face sheet with basic information, although most of the patient's records were in the computer. Heavyset with straight, graying black hair cut chin-length, Keely conveyed her usual air of truculence. "Make sure you check for side effects to her hormones. She's a surrogate."

Harper glanced at the sheet. Vanessa Ayres, age thirty-two. Taking birth control pills to coordinate her cycle.

A wave of unease swept over Harper. What were the

odds of two surrogates at Safe Harbor undergoing the process at the same time? She didn't mean to intrude on anyone's privacy by learning anything further about Mrs. Ayres. "Maybe I'd better not...."

Keely disappeared into an examining room. Given her mercurial temper—although she never vented it on Dr. Brennan, whom she adored—Harper hesitated to call her back.

Did this violate ethics? She'd already seen the name, so it was too late to avoid that. All she had to do was confirm some key points of the medical history, take the woman's vitals, ask about side effects and carry out whatever directions Paige gave.

There wasn't time to consult Nora, who'd left for lunch. Harper might as well perform her duties in a professional manner and be quick about it. Besides, it wasn't the surrogate who'd declined contact with the egg donor. Mrs. Ayres was probably willing to go along with whatever the recipient requested, so Harper wouldn't be breaching *her* rights.

In the waiting room, she called the patient's name. A tall woman—about Harper's height—responded. With reddish-blond hair and a sprinkling of freckles, she bore no other obvious physical resemblance. But then, why should she?

My babies, her uterus. What a weird situation.

As Harper went through the prep, she couldn't help empathizing when she asked about side effects.

"A little bloating," the surrogate reported as she sat on the examining table.

"That must be uncomfortable." *As if I didn't know.*

"I'm too excited to care about that."

"You're enthusiastic about being a surrogate?" Despite Harper's reluctance to pry, the question slipped out. "I suppose you must be, or you wouldn't do it."

"It's been three years since my first one." Vanessa beamed. "She lives in Paris. The family emails me photos on her birthday. She's so cute!"

Harper had heard that many countries, including France, banned surrogacy, with the result that foreign parents came to California for fertility services. The state's laws protected all parties in such arrangements while leaving medical decisions to the individuals.

"Was it your genetic child?" she ventured.

The woman nodded. "My twelve-year-old daughter's thrilled to have a half sister. She plans to study French in high school so they can talk if they ever meet."

Goose bumps rose on Harper's arms. "Your husband's okay with this?"

"In addition to our daughter, he has a twenty-year-old son from his previous marriage." Vanessa's straightforward manner assured Harper that she didn't mind the line of questioning. "He's relieved that I don't insist on enlarging our family, because we can't afford it. I'm sure you're aware how much college costs these days."

"My daughter's only six. Seven," Harper corrected. "We celebrated her birthday last weekend."

"How darling!"

Although tempted to chat further, Harper reined in the impulse. "Let me check on the doctor."

In the hall, Keely said Paige was running late. That wasn't surprising, since the obstetrician never hurried a patient who needed to talk.

Harper popped in to explain to Vanessa, adding, "Would you like me to bring you a magazine from the waiting room? We usually keep some in here, but I don't see... Oh, there's one." She retrieved a maternity magazine from atop a cabinet.

Vanessa regarded the heavily pregnant cover model.

"That'll be me in a few months. It was a joy sharing my pregnancy with Cécile—my first mom. She and Maurice flew here for the ultrasound and late in the pregnancy, to feel the baby move. And of course for the delivery. This round, it's a single dad. I'm curious to see how that will go."

Best not to hear any more. "I'm sure it will work out fine." Harper eased toward the exit.

"He's a great guy." On the examining table, Vanessa wrapped her arms around her upthrust knees. "His wife died and he's too devoted to her to consider marrying again, but he craves children. He's a teacher, and after talking to him, I'm sure he's well prepared for what's involved."

Harper's chest squeezed. What were the odds of there being two men like that in Safe Harbor? She should have left five minutes ago. Or, better, she should have insisted Keely prep this patient.

And she should have suspected that Peter couldn't be as wonderful as he seemed. While pretending to be her friend, he'd been treating her like some object he might purchase. How long had he been considering her as the egg donor? How much of their contact had been a way to assess her suitability? Just thinking about it made Harper furious.

After a light knock, in walked Dr. Brennan, a six-foot-tall redhead who shot her a startled look. "Nurse?" Her sharp tone made it clear this was an inappropriate situation.

She knows. How many other people were aware of the connection between Harper and Peter? Paige, Nora, Zack, even Cole? *Everyone but me, apparently.*

Flushing, Harper hurried out. At the nurses' station, she was grateful to find no one else around.

Thoughts tumbled over one another. What would she

say to Peter on Saturday? Would he find out that she'd talked to Vanessa? What should she do?

While Harper hadn't known *his* identity, he'd obviously known hers. Although the egg donor registry didn't carry full names, clients saw a profile, including a photo. Last Sunday, when Peter heard her discussing her feelings with Cole and Stacy, no wonder he hadn't commented. He'd understood perfectly well what was going on, and had kept it from her.

How could he have deceived her like this? What kind of person was he, anyway?

Fists clenched, she considered marching over to the hospital and telling Melissa she was withdrawing. It would be awkward all the way around, but then, that wasn't her fault. Now that she'd stumbled on the truth, it would be impossible to go through with this procedure while feigning ignorance.

A painfully familiar scene unfolded in Harper's mind. In a green meadow, two little boys were playing...

If she halted the donation at this stage, she might be excluded from the program permanently. Even if Safe Harbor allowed her to remain, what future recipient would choose an egg donor who'd reneged? And how disappointing for Vanessa. She hadn't done anything wrong.

Mostly, Harper hated to abandon those little boys. Sure, she could rationalize that they were mere fantasies. Never real. Never meant to take tangible form. But in her heart, she saw them growing up, tall and strong.

How could Peter do this to her?

Take a deep breath and think it over. She had more sense than to go off half-cocked.

As for the birth control pills, Harper decided to keep taking them for now. To stop abruptly might cause problems, and if she asked Zack about that, she'd have to explain what she'd discovered.

Before anything else, she needed to confront Peter. Maybe he'd have the decency to explain to Melissa that he was responsible for putting Harper in this situation. Then she might not be ousted from the program entirely.

He'd be upset, though. He might claim that keeping her in the dark was a valid choice. If so, they'd argue, and that would be the end of that.

Her gut twisted. After Saturday, Harper wasn't likely to see him again outside sports camp, and by next summer he'd be gone. She'd miss him far too much. And so would her daughter.

I'm an idiot. But how could I have known?

As for Peter, he'd be free to select another donor. A more suitable one, a woman who hadn't been foolish enough to start caring about a man who was only using her.

EMERGING FROM THE HOSPITAL garage on Thursday for his appointment with Dr. Rattigan, Peter wasn't prepared for the wave of emotion that slammed into him. His throat clamped shut until he could scarcely breathe.

He and Angela had come here full of hope, seeking fertility treatment. A few weeks later, after a series of tests, she'd received her shocking diagnosis.

Since her death, Peter had been back several times, experiencing only an undercurrent of sorrowful memories on his way to see Dr. Rattigan. Yesterday, though, had marked the second anniversary of his wife's death. As he did every month, he'd visited the cemetery to put flowers on her grave.

He'd shed a few tears, missing her. He'd recalled happy occasions: their wedding, their honeymoon on Catalina Island, their joy the day escrow closed on their house.

Today, painful memories swamped him. Angela in the last days, her soft brown hair struggling to grow back from chemotherapy, her hazel eyes dull, her body racked with pain. He'd felt so helpless, longing to substitute his strength for her frailty, to carry her out of the hospital and take her home as if, miraculously, being surrounded by her favorite possessions would restore her to health.

Although most of her treatment had occurred at a cancer center, she'd learned the terrible truth here at Safe Harbor. The shock of that first, horrifying discovery, the kindness and sorrow on her doctor's face, the realization that their dreams of parenthood were turning into a nightmare, swept over Peter full force.

For the year after her death, he'd had irrational reactions, half expecting another bolt from the blue—fearful of bad news at his annual checkup, worried when he couldn't immediately reach his parents that they'd been in an accident. Recently, though, he'd been so busy planning for the surrogacy that he'd put all that out of his mind.

He forced himself into motion toward the medical office building. This reaction would pass. And, indeed, the shock began to fade once he reached the lobby. As he rode the elevator to the fourth floor, the lingering sense of dread faded to a ripple of anxiety.

Dr. Rattigan's nurse, a fellow named Lucky with a solid physique and military-style short hair, ushered Peter into a room. No exam today, just a chance to raise questions.

Cole entered moments later, looking far more dignified in his white coat than he had wearing pipe cleaner antennae at Sunday's party. He regarded Peter with a mild frown. Was he wondering about Peter's personal involvement with Harper?

If so, he didn't mention it. With brisk efficiency, he

asked how Peter felt and then reviewed the upcoming medical procedure.

Where other physicians had failed to find the cause of Peter's low sperm count, Cole had determined that he suffered from a rare immunological response. Possibly as a result of a sports-related injury to the testicles during adolescence, his body had begun producing antibodies that killed much of his sperm. Enough remained, however, for him to become a father with the aid of modern technology. Since surrogacy with donor eggs required using in vitro fertilization, anyway, this didn't pose a major additional problem.

"Once the eggs are retrieved from the donor, they'll be taken to the lab." Cole's voice had a smooth tone, as if he'd recited these words many times, which no doubt he had. "The embryologist will inspect them to make sure they appear healthy, and then microsurgically inject the sperm."

"Any risk of a mix-up?" Peter, who remained standing, folded his arms. This might be a clinical procedure but it was intensely personal, as well. "I don't want to find out years later I'm raising some other guy's kids."

"We label eggs and sperm and check their identity at every step," Cole assured him. "In fact, we confirm the ID several times at each stage."

That was reassuring. "Go on."

"The following day, the oocytes—the eggs—will be assessed to determine those that contain two pronuclei, which will indicate fertilization," the urologist continued. "Each pronucleus contains genetic information from one of the parents."

"I figured that out," Peter said dryly.

"Ah, yes, you teach biology," Cole murmured. "Still, I don't want to omit any details."

"I appreciate that."

"We continue to monitor the development of the fertilized oocytes. When they're three days old, they should contain eight cells. At that point, if everything is developing normally, they're ready to be transferred into the surrogate."

"You make it sound so simple," Peter said.

Cole blinked. "Do I? Far from it. The transfer takes careful coordination by a team including the embryologist, the physician and an ultrasound technician. It's done through a catheter while the patient, the surrogate in this case, is awake. She lets the team know if she experiences any cramping."

"What if she does?"

"Mild cramping isn't necessarily a problem, but the doctor will check to be sure the catheter is in the proper position."

"How many embryos would you implant?" Peter asked. "I mean, transfer." He preferred using the correct terminology.

"That's a controversial topic," the doctor said. "Some countries restrict the number of embryos by law to no more than two."

"Why is that any of their business?" Peter flared. "I know multiple pregnancies can be risky. But isn't that the woman's decision?"

"Personally, I suspect some of those countries, which tend to have government-paid medical care, are more concerned about the cost of a high-risk pregnancy," Cole responded. "However, that may be uncharitable of me."

"What about in the U.S.?"

"Doctors are allowed reasonable discretion, although there are guidelines," the doctor said. "A lot depends on the circumstances. In this situation, we would transfer no more than three."

"But we can save the others?"

"Yes. If there are extras, they'll be frozen," Cole agreed. "You can use them later or donate them to other families."

Peter hadn't considered that possibility. "Then someone else would be raising my children."

"This assisted fertility business gets complicated," Cole observed. "Morally as well as medically."

"So it does."

"After the transfer, we'll give you a printed report accounting for every oocyte and embryo," the doctor informed him. "You'll have full information."

"Nothing slipshod about this operation." High standards were one of the reasons Peter had chosen the program, along with up-to-the-minute technology and the convenient location.

"Any more questions?" Cole asked.

Might as well address the subject they'd been avoiding. "What do you think I should do about Harper?"

The urologist appeared to take a mental time-out as he stood considering. Most people would instinctively fill the silence with a flow of words. Not Cole.

That was fine with Peter. He didn't want easy answers.

"Legally and medically, you're within your rights to keep your role a secret," Cole said at last. "But sooner or later she's likely to find out."

"You think so?" Although that possibility had occurred to Peter, he hadn't seen it as inevitable.

"If you socialize with her, she's almost certain to learn that you're having a baby by a surrogate," Cole said. "From there, it's a short hop to connecting the dots."

At some level, Peter had suspected that, as much as he'd tried to persuade himself otherwise. Yet he didn't want to cancel the arrangement. "By the time the surrogate gets pregnant, won't Harper be out of the picture?"

The doctor's expression revealed nothing of his opinion. He must be a killer poker player. "Once the eggs are harvested, her role is finished."

"So I don't have to do anything?" Even as he formed the words, Peter knew he was splitting hairs.

"It depends on whether you care how she feels."

To lose Harper's friendship would be painful; to destroy her respect and trust would be worse. "I do, but these are going to be my kids," he said. "I'm not willing to share custody."

"If she violates her agreement to relinquish the offspring, then she's the one on shaky ethical and legal ground," Cole pointed out. "Although I have to admit, that sort of logic doesn't always carry weight when people's emotions are aroused."

"You think she might sue?"

"If she does, I believe she'd lose," the doctor said. "She signed a contract, and California law is well established on the subject."

That wasn't really Peter's fear, anyway. It had more to do with...well, with what? Seeing the anguish on Harper's face when she fell in love with his child and then had to give it up?

If that was so important to him, he shouldn't have selected her in the first place. But she was the right mother... egg donor. He couldn't imagine choosing anyone else.

"You may be overthinking this," Cole went on. "I've heard her say how much she enjoys having time to spend with Mia and pursue her photography. Women are complicated—Stacy's been giving me an education in that. I guess if you want to find out what they think, the best way is to listen to them."

"First I'd have to tell her."

"That would be a logical deduction."

"And I'm very logical," Peter muttered, although he could see that he'd been nothing of the sort. "Thanks, Doc."

"Anytime." Cole extended his hand, and they shook. "It will be only a few weeks before we move to the next phase of your fatherhood."

Unless Harper shuts the whole thing down. A definite risk if he came clean, Peter conceded.

He'd be seeing her Saturday. By then, he'd make a decision and, one way or the other, prepare to face the consequences.

Chapter Eight

A quiet summons from Nora to meet with her and Paige after hours on Friday filled Harper with dread. She had no doubt what this concerned, now that the two partners had had time to discuss her encounter with the surrogate.

Were they going to fire her? Although both were on staff at the hospital, and therefore under the direction of administrator Dr. Mark Rayburn, they owned their private practice and were her direct employers.

She'd never dreamed that becoming an egg donor might cost her this job. It wasn't fair. But then, medical professionals risked their reputations and sometimes their careers with every decision they made.

That afternoon, Harper arranged with another parent to pick up Mia at sports camp. Not that she minded missing a possible encounter with Peter, whom she'd been avoiding since Wednesday.

By five-thirty, the last patient had been sent on her way with a printed-out summary of medical instructions, and Keely and the receptionist had departed. Squaring her shoulders, Harper went to learn her fate.

They met in Dr. Franco's office. The obstetricians looked nothing alike—blonde, delicate Nora was dwarfed by her flame-haired partner—but both had larger-than-life personalities. Even seated, they overwhelmed the room, with its tidy desk, bookshelves and framed degrees and certificates.

Harper edged inside, staying close to the door as if ready to flee. Well, she *was.*

"I suppose you know what we're here to discuss," Nora said.

Harper nodded. "It was an accident."

"Keely explained how you came to be prepping Mrs. Ayres," Paige said. "You were doing her, and me, a favor."

Despite the encouraging words, Harper went on. "I didn't tell her about my involvement." She wished her tone didn't sound so defensive.

Nora blew out a long breath. "All the same, it's troubling. We haven't reported this to anyone else, but we'll need to." "Anyone else" presumably included Dr. Owen Tartikoff, head of the fertility program, as well as Dr. Rayburn. Harper tried not to think about how scary she found those guys.

"And the recipient will have to be notified," Paige put in.

"I plan to tell Peter myself," Harper informed them. "We're meeting tomorrow to discuss creating a picture book together."

"A picture book?" Nora said. "That sounds like fun."

"Are you guys dating?" Paige shook her head. "Sorry. None of my business. But I can't believe he didn't— I mean, this whole situation…"

"He should have told you," finished her partner, who then added quickly, "I mean, I'm not confirming that he's the father."

"It's obvious," Harper replied. "And if he'd told me himself, we wouldn't be in this jam."

"But we are," Paige said. "Patient confidentiality is primary."

"Which patient's?" Harper put in. "Mrs. Ayres's or Peter's?"

"Since the surrogate has agreed to meet with all parties, we're mainly concerned with the father," Nora replied. "And I consider him partly at fault. He must have been aware of the likelihood of your stumbling on the truth."

The two doctors' eyes met. Apparently they'd discussed this issue between them, and hadn't entirely agreed.

"He might not see it that way," Paige cautioned. "Men tend to compartmentalize more than women do."

"And they always think they're so rational," Nora grumbled.

"Leo acting cranky?" her friend inquired.

"Oh, he's putting in long hours on a difficult case." Nora's husband was an investigator with the Safe Harbor Police Department.

"He could always join Mike's agency," Paige teased. "Then he could work even longer hours for less money and fewer benefits." Her husband, Mike Aaron, co-owned a detective agency.

Nora rolled her eyes. "It's more than my life is worth to suggest such a thing. Leo plans to be chief someday."

Harper clasped her hands and waited for them to return to the subject. Which, noticing her expression, they promptly did.

"Since you're making disclosure to the...possible father," Nora said, "we'll wait till Monday to brief the powers that be."

"You don't think he might sue, do you?" Paige asked.

"If he does, I'll sue him back." Harper's jaw tightened. She had no idea whether she had grounds, but in her opinion, Peter was the one who'd broken *her* trust.

"I'll inform my brother-in-law on Monday, too," Nora

said. Tony Franco served as hospital attorney. "We should have done that earlier."

Again, she and Paige locked gazes. Paige lost the staring contest.

As she left the office, Harper ran through a host of possibilities. What if Peter insisted she go ahead with the egg donation as a condition of his not making trouble? That would be blackmail, but perhaps not from his perspective.

As Dr. Franco had said, men tended to believe they were being rational. Even when they weren't.

DESPITE BEING FAIRLY certain that the book project was a dead issue, Harper slipped out early Saturday with her camera. Sitting on the grass in a rear corner of the yard, she waited and watched in the silver-gray light until a twinkle of orange caught her eye.

The butterfly had large black spots on its orange wings, and a span close to two inches. Carefully, she adjusted her settings and captured its luminous beauty.

"What are you doing, Mommy?"

Mia had reached her with barely a whisper of footsteps, and spoke near her mother's ear. As a result, she didn't frighten away the tiny creature.

"Remember I told you that Peter and I might work on a book?" While Harper regretted having informed her daughter, it was too late to undo that now. "I thought I'd see what I could find."

Mia held up her new camera. "Can I take its picture, too?"

"Of course."

A minute later, after the butterfly rambled off, they searched the internet on Harper's phone for a match. "There it is!" She pointed at an image almost too small to see. "It's called a tortoiseshell."

Scrolling down, Mia gaped at a striped caterpillar. "Oh, my gosh! I nearly stepped on one of those. I almost killed a butterfly baby!"

"Accidents happen." Harper refrained from noting that spiders and cockroaches also had babies, none of which she planned to preserve.

They took more photos, capturing a leafhopper, a nearly translucent spider and a common housefly. Then it was time to drive Mia to the ceramics workshop. Returning half an hour before her appointment with Peter, Harper set out coffee mugs and blueberry muffins.

She wasn't sure why she went to so much trouble for a man who'd betrayed her. Still, he deserved a chance to explain.

She smacked her hand on the counter. *Stop being so darn nice, Harper!* The man had insinuated himself into her life—not without an invitation, true—but he'd endeared himself under false pretenses to her and to Mia. Especially Mia.

Couldn't he see how fragile her daughter's heart was? Although Mia seemed sturdy, Harper knew her daughter longed to be part of a family. She'd asked three times why Uncle Jake didn't call or send a present. They hadn't heard from him, even though Harper had emailed her brother a chatty message several weeks earlier with a reminder about his niece's birthday.

Then, all week, Mia had brimmed with happy observations of what Peter said and did at sports camp. He'd become an important part of her emotional landscape.

Harper wished he weren't moving. And that he hadn't proposed this book without telling her he'd hired her as the egg donor. And that... Oh, heck, she was too old and too jaded to make wishes that couldn't come true.

The doorbell chose that inconvenient moment to ring. He *would* have to be on time.

Grumpily, Harper went to answer.

PETER HAD RESOLVED TO steer the conversation carefully. Instead, words failed him as he stared into the snapping green eyes of the woman who'd dominated his thoughts.

In a folder, he held a printed outline of the book, along with information regarding publishers and the self-publishing process. By starting on neutral ground, he'd intended to ease into the tricky topic that refused to remain a secret.

Instead, he stood on the porch while she glared at him. "What's wrong?" he asked.

"We need to talk." Harper moved stiffly from his path.

Nothing unusual had happened at sports camp, nor was he late today. Could her attitude result from the birth control pills? Concerned for her health, Peter had read up on those, and learned that they might affect her moods.

When he entered, the enchanting scent of baking enveloped him. "That smells wonderful."

"I made muffins for Mia." Almost snarling, she added, "There are a few left." With that, Harper stalked to the kitchen.

Peter followed, concerned but beginning to be irked by her attitude. When he misstepped with Angela, a smile and a quiet discussion had always smoothed things over. He was a reasonable man.

Refreshments were already set out on the table. Po skittered about on the tiled floor until Harper scooped him up, petted him and carried him to the laundry room. Peter could hear her murmuring, "I don't want to step on you, baby. You'll be fine in here."

Any hope that her mood might be mellowing, however,

faded when she returned. Although she'd ceased glaring, her jaw was clamped shut.

Peter indicated the food. "This, uh... Thanks."

Harper washed her hands and joined him. Not eating or drinking. Or saying, "You're welcome," either.

"Is this like the last meal of a condemned man?" he asked.

She blinked. "I beg your pardon?"

"I've done something to make you angry," he said. "What, exactly?"

"Guess."

He was trying to be polite, while she insisted on making this difficult. "Why don't you just tell me?"

"I met someone this week," Harper replied. "A patient named Vanessa Ayres."

Peter's hands went cold. "I meant to tell you."

"When?"

"Today." He resented being treated like a criminal. "But I was under no obligation to reveal my identity."

"You nearly got me fired!" Tears glimmered behind the anger. "I still might be! When I prepped Vanessa, I had no way of knowing she was your surrogate or that you were using my eggs. Now I've breached patient confidentiality. That's a serious offense."

Regret crowded out his annoyance. "Mrs. Ayres isn't seeing the doctor you work for." He'd checked on that as a precaution.

"No—just her partner!" Harper cried. "The nurses help each other when the office gets busy."

He could see now how naive he'd been. Willfully blind, to be more accurate. "How did she react?"

"I didn't tell her." Harper pressed her lips so tightly they turned white.

Peter ran his fingers through his hair, a nervous gesture

that Angela had cured him of long ago. Or so he'd believed. "I didn't expect for you to find out like this."

"You didn't expect for me to find out at all!"

On the verge of arguing, he halted. "You're right, I didn't. Until a couple of days ago, when I had a talk with my doctor. With Cole." Might as well come clean about that, as well.

She folded her arms. "Are you going to sue me?"

The idea had never occurred to him. "Certainly not."

"Even if I withdraw?"

A dark knot formed in Peter's gut. He could have other children, but he wanted *hers*. And to keep her friendship. Impulsively, he reached across the table to touch her hand. "Please don't give up on me."

"I should!" But she didn't jerk away.

"And I'd deserve it."

Apparently he'd said the right thing, because her forehead smoothed. "What on earth were you thinking, choosing me in the first place?"

He let the truth spill out. "That you're a wonderful mother and you have an adorable child. And that it would mean a lot that my children came from you." He explained about recognizing her at sports camp, returning to the website and reaching his conclusion. "I didn't realize initially that we'd be seeing this much of each other."

"When you signed the papers to hire me, you should have told me. It would have been the decent thing to do."

She had a good point. "Look, I tend to be reserved, which means I don't always communicate well," Peter admitted. "When there's a lot at stake, I weigh things carefully."

"Not carefully enough." She shook her head. "Okay, that was uncalled for. But it feels like you took advantage of me."

Had he? Not intentionally, Peter thought. "I believed…well, convinced myself that it didn't matter, since you'd agreed to donate eggs without meeting the parents. I can see now I was wrong."

She stared down at the table, clearly fighting her emotions. This had affected her strongly, and that bothered him, a lot.

"Do you want me to write to your doctors taking all the responsibility?" Peter asked. "You really think they might fire you?"

"It's possible." She swallowed. "Even a reprimand in my file could hurt my future prospects."

"Say the word and I'll write to them, or call them, or both."

"Okay. It might help."

She hadn't said whether she intended to go ahead with providing eggs. Did he dare discuss the subject further? As Peter had said, he tended to be reticent in important matters. Speaking up risked encouraging her to withdraw.

On the other hand, keeping quiet had caused nothing but trouble. "May I tell you what I'm most afraid of?" he asked. "It's the reason I didn't tell you sooner."

Harper swallowed, and then met his gaze. "Go ahead." The jut of her chin indicated she was reserving judgment.

"These are the children I dreamed of having with Angela," Peter said. "This was our journey, and then cancer tore us apart. I lost her. I can't lose them, too. I was afraid that if you were involved with the pregnancy and saw the baby or babies, you wouldn't be able to let go."

For a moment, she showed no reaction. Then she surprised him by saying, "Let me tell you my dream."

He reminded himself to breathe. "Please do."

"It's a real dream." She ducked her head. "I mean, it's

not a wish or a fantasy, it's something that comes to me while I'm sleeping. Over and over."

With no idea where this might be heading, Peter merely waited.

"I'm out in a field." Harper studied her clasped hands. They were pretty hands, with long tapered fingers and lightly polished nails. She'd moved her wedding ring to the right side, he noted. "There are two boys playing. Sometimes they're toddlers, other times they might be five or six."

"Two boys?" he repeated.

A quick nod. "There's a shadowy figure playing with them. A man, but I can't make out his face. They're playing catch, or tag—it varies."

"I see." But he didn't.

"Nobody realizes I'm there, and I think that's because I'm not." Although tears glittered on her lashes, Harper met Peter's gaze squarely. "I have the sense that I'm meant to give them life. That's all. They won't be *my* sons. They're supposed to be born and I'm supposed to make that happen."

"And let them go."

"Exactly."

He'd never realized her involvement was so powerful— or so unselfish. "Angela, I'm sorry."

"You called me Angela."

"What?" He had, he realized with a guilty pang. "I mean, Harper, I'm sorry. I should have trusted you."

"You love these little guys, even though they don't exist yet," she observed.

He had no way to express the emotions swelling inside him, except to say, "I do."

"Me, too, but not the same way." Harper fiddled with the cup of coffee that she hadn't touched until now. "Still, it's a good thing you're moving. You're right. I might start to get attached if I watched them grow up. But, Peter, I'm prepared to say goodbye to them. That's what I've intended from the beginning, and I'll stick with it, if you still want my eggs."

She was leaving the decision to him? Withdrawing wasn't an option, from Peter's perspective. Not that he believed in premonitions, exactly, yet her dream made these "little guys," as she put it, all the more real.

"Absolutely," he said.

Her shoulders relaxed. "I understand that it's your journey with Angela. Some people are bonded for a lifetime. I don't know if that's the case with you...."

"I believe it is."

"It wasn't for me," Harper went on. "I miss Sean, but for me, the journey continues without him. As for being an egg donor, this is just one leg of the trip. Once it's over, you'll leave and Mia and I will have new adventures. I only hope she won't grow too attached."

"To me or the babies?"

"Both." Frowning, she said, "I'm trying not to discuss the process too much with her. It's difficult, though."

Peter wasn't sure how to keep the little girl at arm's length. She was so cute, he couldn't help being fond of her. "I guess we should explain about my plans to leave."

"I'll do it," Harper told him. "And while we're working on the book, we need to be careful around her not to act as if we're co-parenting."

"You're right." Peter would rather not pull back from Mia. Still, Harper was right. "Now where do we go from here?"

"In terms of the book or the babies?"

"Both," he said.

Harper indicated the folder. "Why don't you show me what's in there, and we'll figure it out."

It seemed a good place to start. "Here's how I thought we'd organize it," he began, and took out the papers.

Chapter Nine

Grateful though she was for their forthright discussion, Harper kept one fact to herself: that, strangely enough, it wasn't the prospect of giving up the babies that hurt most. It was the reminder that, in his heart, Peter belonged to his late wife, and always would.

However, she accepted that. *It's not as if I wasn't warned.*

And now that they'd moved past the touchy issues, Peter was bursting with ideas for their book. He radiated excitement as they reviewed his outline and discussed how to see insects from a child's perspective. He praised her new photos and the pictures Mia had shot, as well.

"Why not use both?" Peter asked. "Not for every insect, but we could incorporate her images and comments here and there. It brings a whole new dimension."

"Make her a co-author?" What a valuable experience for Mia. "That's a great idea."

"She'll deserve a third of the earnings, assuming there are any," Peter said with a lopsided grin.

"For her education fund." Harper could have hugged him. Well, almost.

She decided to consider the next few months as a special period—limited and unique, a time when babies might grow and a book take shape. By next summer, this part of her life would be over. She planned to cherish every moment, and then, like a butterfly from its cocoon, leave it behind.

"What do you think about breaking up some of the text into sections that will fit inside boxes?" he asked. "It'll help hold the reader's attention."

"And it's visually appealing, too." Returning her attention to the printout, Harper bent her head close to his and went to work.

"LOOKIT! LOOKIT! LOOKIT!" Inside the Bear and Doll Boutique, Mia raised her cell phone to take pictures of a shelf of bears costumed as fairy tale characters. "Can we use these, Mommy?"

Harper laughed. Every morning that week, they'd arisen early to catch the insects unawares. "Honey, we aren't writing a book about bears."

"I'll make my own book, like Peter showed us." Mia had saved the instruction sheet from her birthday party.

"Good idea." Harper guided her daughter out of the path of several older children. The store was crowded today because the proprietor, Mrs. Humphreys, was holding a youth workshop on how to make doll clothes.

At the counter, Harper paid her daughter's fee. "Are you sure it's all right to leave Mia here for an hour?" she asked the cheerful older woman who'd been a friend of Harper's mother. "I'll be a few doors down at A Memorable Decor."

"She'll do fine," Ada assured her. "I'm happy to keep an eye on her."

Once Mia was settled, Harper checked her watch. It was nearly 10:00 a.m., when she'd arranged to meet Stacy at the antiques store. In addition to furnishings, it carried vintage clothing and had just received a shipment of bridal gowns.

She found her friend waiting in a narrow aisle lined

with desks, mirrors and ottomans. "I peeked already," Stacy noted as they wended their way to the rear of the shop. "You'd be surprised how relaxed some of the waist-lines are."

"I guess they had pregnant brides in the old days, too." Harper noticed how markedly her friend's bulge had grown in the two weeks since the birthday party. Three babies meant triple the expansion.

"Not such old days." Stacy checked a descriptive tag. "This is from the 1970s. The hippie era."

"Forty years ago! That's old," Harper said.

"Look at this one." Stacy lifted down an elegant dress with cap sleeves and a high waist.

A saleslady appeared at her elbow. "Shall I put that in a dressing room for you?"

"Yes, please."

Spotting a couple of dresses on another rack, Harper went to investigate. "This is beautiful." She lifted down a Grecian-style gown with a wrapped empire waistline. Whirling, she couldn't resist holding it against herself.

"Oh, my goodness, are you getting married? Congrat-ulations."

Startled, she met the friendly gaze of the woman she'd last seen on an examining table: Vanessa Ayres. "Uh, hello."

"Funny how I keep running into you." The surrogate spread her hands expressively. "Peter Gladstone called a few days ago to explain that you're the egg donor and to apologize for putting us both in such a ticklish position. I was hoping we'd have a chance to talk."

"And here we are." As good as his word, Peter had taken the initiative in straightening out matters, with Vanessa and with the hospital administrators. On Monday, Harper had been on edge until Nora reassured her that all was well, although the hospital's attorney had complained about the delay in informing him.

"This is beautiful." The strawberry-blonde fingered the chiffon fabric.

"It's not for me," Harper said. "Stace?"

Her friend swung around from the row of dresses. "Hello?"

Harper made introductions and explained that Stacy was also an egg donor. That prompted her friend, who seemed to feel no embarrassment on the subject, to disclose that she'd accidentally become pregnant the same month the eggs were harvested.

"If you're getting married, things must have worked out, or am I assuming too much?" Vanessa responded.

"Things have definitely worked out." Stacy's gaze fell on the Grecian dress. "I love that!"

Harper handed it over. "Try it on."

"You bet."

Since the dressing room was the size of an old-fashioned phone booth, Harper waited outside. "Don't let me interrupt your shopping," she told Vanessa.

"I'm killing time while my daughter's sewing doll clothes." The surrogate smoothed her palm over an embroidered runner on a table.

"So is mine." Feeling awkward with this unfamiliar relationship, Harper searched for a way to continue the conversation. "I'd have stayed with her but I promised to help Stacy."

"I'd have stayed, too, but now that she's twelve, Sarella doesn't want her mommy hanging around." The other woman shrugged. "It's lucky I can go on having babies. That satisfies my maternal instincts so I don't cling."

"Sarella," Harper repeated. "What a pretty name."

"She hates it." Vanessa gave her an ironic smile. "She wishes we'd named her after the latest teen idol."

"I'm glad Mia hasn't reached that stage yet."

Silence fell. Elsewhere in the store, a young couple raised and lowered the side bar on a crib, while two older women lifted teacups and examined the bottoms.

"I wonder if he's planning ahead for when he has grand-children." Harper indicated a middle-aged man testing a rocking chair.

"I'm certainly not going to ask him," Vanessa replied in a low voice.

"Maybe he just has trouble falling asleep."

"I'm not going to ask him that, either."

They chuckled. Harper was wondering if she should poke her head into the dressing room when Stacy emerged in the Grecian gown. Supported by a single strap on one side, it flattered her figure and her complexion.

"Well?" She examined herself in a cheval glass. "It's perfect, isn't it?"

"Absolutely the best yet," Harper said.

"Gorgeous," Vanessa agreed.

Grinning, Stacy ducked back into the dressing room.

"How romantic," Vanessa said dreamily. "I love every-thing about weddings."

"I may not love everything about them," Harper admit-ted. "But Stacy deserves this, especially after her terrible first marriage."

"I'm sure he was a complete jerk."

"You don't know the half of it," she said. "But yes."

"How lovely to meet her, and chat with you." The sur-rogate removed a veil from a hat tree, turning it in her hands to examine the lace. "We're companions in arms, doing something marvelous together."

"It seemed presumptuous of me to get in touch with you

directly, though," Harper said. "I mean, because I work in your doctor's office."

"Who cares?" Vanessa replaced the veil. "A surrogate's medical details aren't exactly a secret."

That reminded Harper of something she'd been wondering. "By the way, do you expect to attend my procedure?" The retrieval was scheduled for Tuesday, with the transfer on Friday. "I don't know what the, uh, etiquette is."

"Etiquette?" Vanessa's eyebrows rose.

"What's customary," Harper amended. "Since you've done this before, you're the expert."

Vanessa laughed. "I'm far from an expert." The surrogate appeared more relaxed with this topic than Harper was. "As for etiquette, there isn't any. We may not be the very first women to interact this way, but we *are* pioneers. That means we're making up the rules as we go."

That was an aspect of this process that Harper hadn't considered. "You're right. This is a new area." There was no established way for the mother of the eggs to relate to the surrogate carrying her baby for a third party. Not many years ago, this would have been the stuff of science fiction.

"I'm keeping a scrapbook for the baby," Vanessa went on. "Pictures of my pregnancy and so on. That way, he'll have a complete record, like any other child."

"That's very thoughtful." Knowing how much Mia enjoyed reviewing her baby book, Harper admired Vanessa's kindness. "I don't plan to have anyone take pictures of me injecting myself with hormones, though." After finishing the birth control pills, she'd moved on to this new phase. So far, her reactions had consisted of soreness in her bottom from the needle and tenderness in her abdomen.

"Ouch!" The surrogate touched her wrist. "You're a brave woman."

"And you aren't?"

"Pregnancy is as old as mankind," Vanessa reminded her. "Donating eggs isn't."

"Funny that we call it donating, even though we get paid." Harper knew she was rattling on, but she preferred not to dwell on the medical aspects of what she was doing. Just thinking about it made her wince.

"You're being paid for your time and discomfort, which is a polite term for *pain,*" the other woman answered. "Not for the eggs themselves."

Nevertheless, Harper wished she didn't have to take money from Peter. But he'd assured her it had been set aside long ago and, with college tuitions soaring, Mia's fund needed the boost.

The dressing room curtains parted and Stacy emerged with the dress folded over her arm. "You deserve every penny of that money."

Had she heard the entire conversation? Harper wondered. "Were we talking too loud?"

"Not loud enough. I had to strain really hard."

"You of all people understand what we mean." Vanessa's goodwill bathed the three of them in a shared sense of sisterhood. "I'm glad you found a dress."

"By next month, we may have to decorate a wheelbarrow with satin and lace to trundle me down the aisle, but I'll feel like a Greek goddess," Stacy responded cheerfully.

"Like Aphrodite," the surrogate suggested. "The goddess of procreation."

"Was she?" Stacy yielded the dress to the saleslady. "I'm fuzzy on my mythology."

"Aphrodite was also known as Venus." Vanessa strolled with them to the register. "I'm named after her, according to my mother."

"Appropriately," Harper noted.

"Isn't Venus the one who's always painted naked?" Stacy ignored a startled glance from the saleslady.

"And with perfect boobs," Vanessa said.

Stacy made a face. "Don't remind me. Mine are starting to hurt."

"Developing milk ducts," the surrogate said.

"Too much information." Harper preferred to focus on the dress, which the red-faced clerk was hurriedly wrapping. "Does it need alterations?"

"Maybe a few. Good thing my mom's coming," Stacy replied. "She'll take care of that. No sense altering it till the last minute, anyway, since my body keeps changing."

After she departed, Harper and Vanessa walked to the doll boutique. A couple of cyclists, wearing helmets and bending low over their racing bikes, passed them on the adjacent trail.

"You're welcome to attend the transfer, if it's all right with Peter," Vanessa said.

Startled, Harper had to think about that. "Thanks for the offer, but I think I'll beg off. Unless it's important to you."

"I'm fine either way." Although about the same height, they had different strides. The other woman sped up to match her pace. "The way Peter talks about you, I gathered that you're friends."

"My late husband used to work with him," Harper said. "And he knows my daughter from sports camp."

"Oh." Vanessa didn't probe further.

Harper wasn't about to mention the book project. Vanessa's romantic attitude reminded her of how easily people might make assumptions. After Peter left, Harper didn't want others assuming she must be brokenhearted.

Anyway, they'd reached the boutique. And inside, Mia's eager face filled her with joy.

Harper had her family. And soon, with luck, Peter would have his, too.

THE PHOTOS WERE STUNNING. A ladybug snacking on an aphid, a grasshopper struggling to free itself from a spiderweb—Harper had outdone herself.

"Incredible." Although she'd offered to email him the pictures, Peter was glad she'd saved them until Sunday afternoon so they could review them together, along with shots by her daughter. "Harper, you're incredibly talented, and I'm sure it took a lot of patience to capture these moments."

"What about mine?" demanded the little girl who sat between them at the kitchen table.

"They make a wonderful complement, Mia. That means they go well with your mom's pictures." That gave Peter an idea. "I'd like to include some tips for children on taking their own photos. Mia, you can help me with ideas."

"I like that." Harper's approval warmed him.

"Yes!" Mia wiggled happily. "Can I show you my book? I wrote one, too."

"You bet." Amused, he watched as she squirmed out of the chair and ducked beneath the table. She crawled across his legs and sprinted off.

"Mia!" Harper called. "That was rude. You can't climb all over people."

About to speak in the girl's defense, Peter stopped himself. Although it was tempting to indulge the child, he shouldn't interfere.

"Sorry." Mia's voice drifted back as she ran into the hall.

"I hope she didn't stomp on you too hard," Harper murmured.

"I got stomped a lot worse in my wrestling days." With Mia out of earshot, he seized on the chance to talk privately. Rereading the information about the side effects of egg donation, Peter had found his concerns growing. "Are you feeling okay? I didn't give enough thought to what I was asking of you, taking all those hormones."

"You didn't ask me. I volunteered." From beneath long lashes, Harper regarded him coolly. "I'm a big girl, Peter. I'm fine."

"You don't like being fussed over," he interpreted.

"Guess not." She tapped the mouse.

"Still, the potential impacts aren't minor." Some egg donors experienced complications such as hyperstimulated ovaries, which could swell painfully.

"Dr. Sargent monitors me closely."

Why was she defensive? Peter only wanted to protect her. "There can be bleeding from the procedure next week, too."

"There are always risks with minor surgery." Harper shook back her brown hair, which was growing into an appealingly thick tumble. "You aren't expecting to be there, are you?"

He blinked at the change of gears. "Do you want me to?"

"No!"

"Then I won't." Just as well. He'd rather not witness the procedure unless she needed him, which she clearly didn't. As fascinating as he found biology, Peter disliked anything to do with surgery, which was one reason he hadn't considered going to medical school. "Did I mention that I spoke to the surrogate about you?"

"I know—I ran into her yesterday." Harper's tone softened. "I'm glad you told her."

"How'd it go?"

"To say that we bonded might be exaggerating," she mused. "But we're on the same wavelength."

"Where did you run into—" He broke off as Mia appeared with a printed-out booklet featuring photos of teddy bears. She'd written a brief story, as well, which she read aloud.

"That's wonderful," Peter told her. "You should be proud of writing your own book."

"I am!" She jumped up. "Can I go play with my kitten?"

"Of course," Harper said.

"I'm going to write a book about Po next," the girl announced, and dashed off.

"She's quite creative," Peter said.

"I wish she had grandparents to share her work with." Harper rested her cheek on her fist.

"She has your friends. They seem like a second family." Peter was slightly envious of her intimacy with Stacy and Adrienne. Although he'd formed casual friendships at work and through volunteer activities, he'd never truly felt close to anyone other than his parents and Angela. And, to a degree, Harper.

"No one adores you like a grandparent. Well, not Sean's mother. Oh, never mind that." She indicated his tablet computer. "I'm eager to see what you've been working on."

"I started with bees." Peter opened a passage he'd written. "Shall I read it aloud? I've heard that's a good way to see if it's flowing well."

"Sure." Harper listened raptly, smiling and nodding in places he'd hoped would be amusing. Except for a dangling modifier and one pronoun with a questionable antecedent, she pronounced it perfect. "I'm fascinated by your research," she said after he finished. "I didn't realize bees were the only insects that produce food for people, or that they communicate by dancing."

"Scientists disagree, however, as to whether it's the tango or the cha-cha," Peter deadpanned.

Laughing, Harper punched him lightly in the arm. "Silly."

He'd like to try one of those dances with her, Peter thought. Preferably a waltz, slow and gentle, his body brushing her temptingly rounded contours, his mouth close to her parted lips.

Mia raced into the room, right behind her kitten. She was holding up her camera, trying to snap a picture. A timely interruption, Peter acknowledged. He'd been enjoying his fantasy a little too much.

"You'll get a blur if you shoot while you're moving," Harper told her daughter.

Mia halted in her tracks. "Listen to Mommy, Po. Stop running!" The kitten halted, regarding her quizzically. "Gotcha!" She took the shot, then scooped up the kitten and carried him onto the patio.

"That cat has no idea he's about to be immortalized in a book," Peter said.

"I'm sure he'd be much more cooperative if he did." Harper gazed fondly after the child. "If only I could freeze time. Vanessa's daughter is twelve and she's already acting like a teenager. I'd rather keep Mia this age as long as possible."

It struck Peter that, in less than a week, his own child might begin life. Perhaps a girl like Mia.

"What's running through your mind?" Harper asked.

He frowned. "I didn't say anything."

"You have an expressive face."

He'd always considered himself a guarded person. But then, his wife used to read him fairly well, too. "Next week—well, it's hard not to get excited about it, although I don't want to count too much on the first attempt."

"Me, neither." Harper's fingers tapped the table. "I'll be on pins and needles till we find out."

"Good thing my sister's wedding is next weekend." Peter was flying East on Friday evening. "That ought to keep me from dwelling on this. Plus, while I'm there, I can get a sense of the area."

Since it was a short trip, he'd decided not to contact Angela's family, who lived a few hours' drive away in Virginia. Once he moved to the area, there'd be plenty of time to reconnect.

Then he noticed the strain on Harper's face. "I'm sure you'll find a beautiful house." The words crackled with tension.

"I'm not buying anything yet," he said.

"It would be rather early, I suppose."

"And I'll be back next Monday, well before we get Vanessa's results." He'd reserved an evening flight on Sunday.

"You'll only be there two days?" Harper asked. "That's not much time for such a long trip. Can't you take a few days off from sports camp?"

"I feel a responsibility, especially these last few weeks." The camp ended in late August.

"It's nearly over?" She let out a long breath. "The summer's flying by."

"Too fast," Peter agreed. "Once school starts, I'll have a busy schedule." Between grading papers, preparing for class and assisting the wrestling coach, he rarely had a free day. "We'd better put in as much work on the book as we can before then."

They set an appointment for the weekend after next. As he left—with a farewell hug from Mia—Peter almost regretted not pushing to be present at the egg retrieval. But that would mean intruding into a very personal procedure. Besides, Harper had said no.

Reaching his car, he paused to study her house. What a profusion of flowers out front. And, inside, a vibrant, captivating, sometimes maddening woman, along with a girl and a kitten who were both growing fast.

Like Harper, Peter wished he could freeze or at least slow time. He felt as if, given the speed with which everything was changing, he might return from Maryland to find Mia a teenager and Harper sharing her kitchen table with another man.

Nonsense. He'd only be gone a few days. All the same, Peter lifted his cell phone and snapped a picture.

Chapter Ten

Harper floated into consciousness, groggy from the sedative. The last thing she remembered was being wheeled into the second-floor retrieval room and seeing Zack Sargent's welcoming expression. The doctor had assured her that all systems were go.

An anesthesiologist must have administered the sedative, because after that she'd dozed. Vaguely, she recalled a few sharp pangs when Zack inserted the ultrasound-guided needle to draw the eggs from her ovaries…nothing more.

"You're a champ." The bedside voice belonged to Stacy, Harper discovered when she rolled her head. "Fourteen eggs."

Fourteen. No wonder Harper still felt bloated. Thank goodness Stacy had volunteered to drive her home, pick up Mia and fix dinner. "I'm glad you're here." The words slurred.

"My last surgery ended half an hour ago." As a scrub nurse, Stacy began her day early and finished by three-thirty or four o'clock. "Zack just popped in to talk to you, but you were still sleeping. He'd have preferred to give you the good news himself, only he has another retrieval scheduled."

"Busy program." Harper's voice sounded thick. Why

had she never realized how hard it was to pronounce the letters *b* and *p?*

"You know the postprocedure drill." Stacy recounted the instructions. "No driving or strenuous activities for the rest of the day."

"Cancel the skydiving session."

"I postponed it till tomorrow," came the cheerful rejoinder. "Oh, be sure to report any excessive bleeding."

"Ugh." The mention made Harper's abdomen twinge.

"No important decisions while you're under the influence," Stacy added. "Except for a few documents I brought, signing over all your worldly possessions."

"That won't get you far."

"I half expected Peter to show up," she said. "I guess I'll share the news about the eggs when I see him at sports camp."

"Won't Cole tell him? Or Zack?"

"Probably, but I can't be sure. Cole doesn't discuss patients with me, of course."

"Well, phooey." Harper's eyelids drifted shut.

"Wakey wakey." Stacy shook her gently. "Say, you haven't mentioned who you're inviting to my wedding as your plus-one."

"Mia." That was a given.

"She gets a separate invitation." Stacy began removing Harper's clothes from the storage bag. "Why not Peter?"

"Because we're not—" blearily, Harper searched for the right word "—dating."

"Who're you going to dance with?" Stacy demanded. "Dr. Tartikoff?"

"Spare me." The head of the fertility program, who was serving as Cole's best man, terrified the staff, except when he condescended to charm them, which he did occasionally. "There's Lucky." Cole's male nurse was the other groomsman.

Stacy shook the wrinkles out of Harper's blouse. "He isn't your type."

Harper searched for another objection. "Peter already has a wedding this weekend. His sister's."

"I'm not getting married till next month. Men are allowed to attend more than one ceremony per year." Clearly, Stacy wasn't taking no for an answer. "And you'll look so smashing in your bridesmaid's dress, he'll completely forget what's-her-name."

"His wife?" What a preposterous idea. "He loves her, and always will. It's a passion that will last through slime."

"Time."

"I knew that was the wrong word." Her brain really was muddled.

"He's in denial," her pal told her. "At the birthday party, he couldn't take his eyes off you."

"Except for the bugs. And the children. And the refreshments."

"Never mind those." Stacy short-circuited further argument by asking, "Are you strong enough to get dressed?"

"I don't suppose they'll let me spend the night here." Tentatively, Harper sat up. Her head spun, and then settled. That left her stomach mildly queasy, a familiar sensation from the pills and injections.

That was finished now. She'd done her part. As for what might happen if this attempt didn't work, she was in no mood to dwell on that. Putting one foot in front of the other was a big enough challenge to contemplate.

A nurse joined them. After the routine questions concerning how Harper felt, the woman presented her discharge papers and repeated the instructions Stacy had given. "I admire what you're doing," she concluded. "You and Stacy both. Wow!"

"Thanks." With an effort, Harper swung onto the edge of the bed.

"I hope they'll deliver the babies here at Safe Harbor," the woman chattered on. "I can't wait to see them."

"It'll be a while," Stacy said dryly. Once the nurse left, she helped Harper slide off her gown, and handed over her underwear. "I'm glad you agreed to let me invite Peter to the wedding. That'll be fun."

"I didn't."

"Sure you did."

Had she? With the sedative fogging her brain, Harper wasn't sure. "I think you're tricking me."

"For your own good," Stacy insisted. "Allow me to play Cupid, okay? I love romance."

"I'm not interested in remarrying." Stacy pulled on the loose-fitting pants she'd brought. "Especially not—"

"Your bra's on backward."

"That's impossible."

"I'd have thought so."

Harper glanced down at the sports bra, not much more than a strip of fabric she'd chosen for today because it was easy to manage. She really had put it on backward. "Well, what do you know."

A flurry of shrugging and tugging rectified the mistake. Finally, she was ready to totter out on Stacy's arm, her body aching and her mind rambling.

The next few hours slipped by in a fog. After a nap, Harper welcomed her daughter's return and enjoyed sharing a pizza and antipasto salad with Stacy. Unfortunately, her abdomen hurt.

"Take the pain pills," her friend advised.

"Not yet." Harper didn't want to doze off until Mia's bedtime. "We're going to watch cartoons."

Stacy fixed a mock-stern gaze on Mia. "Take care of your mom."

"When can I see the babies?"

The two women exchanged startled glances. "Uh-oh," Harper said. "I did explain the whole thing, honestly."

"You set up the cartoons," Stacy ordered. "Mia and I will put away the food and have a chat."

Harper didn't try to listen. It felt good to have someone else make explanations for a change.

After Stacy went home, Mia sat in the living room wearing a solemn expression. "I'm glad Fiona's daddy is taking care of the eggs."

What? Oh, right, Alec Denny, embryologist. "He's good at his job."

"And they won't hatch—I mean, be born till spring, like baby chicks," her daughter went on. "Except there's no guarantee, whatever that means."

Oh, dear. Harper decided not to pursue the matter tonight. She was poised to start the cartoons when the bell rang.

"Stacy must have forgotten something."

Mia sprinted for the door and threw it open. "Hi… Peter!"

He'd come. Despite her best intentions, Harper's spirits soared. He hadn't taken her role for granted, or ducked out of the painful aftermath. She yearned to throw her arms around him…and then smack him for putting her through this, which was totally irrational. Peter hadn't put her through anything. She'd volunteered, as she herself had pointed out.

Besides, men were like that. After Mia's birth, while Harper lay throbbing from eight hours of being squeezed in a vise, Sean had strutted around the hospital, boasting that he'd produced a gorgeous baby. She'd only heard that later, though, and by then she'd been in a forgiving mood.

Peter entered shyly, blond hair falling across his forehead, and gave Harper a questioning look. "How're you feeling?"

"Like a pincushion," she admitted, thankful to be wearing a loose, Mexican-style embroidered dress rather than her bathrobe.

He held up a sack. "I had a devil of a time figuring out what kind of present to bring."

Mia skipped over and tried to peek inside. "What is it?"

"It's for you both." Peter drew out a box decorated with a picture of a glass tube filled with red liquid. "It's a hummingbird feeder. There's enough light for me to hang it on your patio now, if that's okay."

"I'd appreciate it." Harper shifted position, and flinched. "I won't be able to help, though."

"You're hurting." He touched her arm. "What can I do?"

How lovely that he was asking, rather than ordering her to bed or demanding she swallow a pill. "Help me onto the patio. You can keep Mia entertained, and I'll watch."

"I can help, too!" Mia came around Harper's far side. Although leaning on them both, at different heights, presented a challenge, Harper braced one hand on her daughter's shoulder and relaxed as Peter's arm surrounded her.

This was what she'd been longing for, without acknowledging it. A man to lean on, just for a while.

At a shuffling pace, they passed through the kitchen, switched on the patio lights and went out. Peter eased Harper onto the couchlike glider, while Mia propped a cushion behind her. "Where'd you learn to do that?" Harper asked.

"Aunt Stacy showed me when she was babysitting,"

Mia replied proudly. "That's what nurses do when your back hurts."

"Now I'll show you what handymen and -women do," Peter said. "I'd fetch a tool kit from my car but I'm betting there's a better one in your garage."

"Sean could have set up a home repair business out there," Harper confirmed, and let Mia show him the way.

While they were gone, twilight settled around her, filled with the twitter of birds and the appetizing scent of the neighbors' grill. The dry climate kept mosquitoes to a minimum, thank goodness. For once, she had no desire to commune with insects.

The pair returned, bringing the tool kit along with a footstool for Mia. More comfortable than she'd felt in days, Harper leaned back to watch the show.

Peter started by hanging an S-hook from a patio-cover slat. "We'll slip the handle over this, and it'll hang at the right height."

"Can't we set it on the table?" Mia asked.

"Putting it up high will discourage squirrels and raccoons from poaching," he told her.

Her face scrunched. "We don't have 'coons, do we, Mommy?"

"I've heard Carolyn mention seeing them." The young secretary from the fertility office lived down the block with her parents.

Mia didn't appear convinced. "How would 'coons get the juice out?"

"You'd be surprised what they can do with their tiny hands, including squeeze milk cartons and turn doorknobs." From the box, Peter lifted a clear plastic tube and a flavor envelope. "Here's a packet of nectar. Let's go mix it with water."

Mia climbed down from her stool. "Do we have any more of that?"

"I brought a recipe for homemade nectar," Peter said as the two of them went inside. "It's one part sugar to four parts water. Don't use honey. It can ferment and kill the hummers."

"What makes it red?" Mia's voice drifted from the kitchen.

"Food coloring, but you shouldn't use that once we've finished this commercial stuff." Through the open window, Harper listened as Peter ran the tap and explained that the effects of red dye on birds hadn't been tested. "You can store leftover nectar in the fridge for two weeks."

"I won't 'member," Mia said worriedly.

"I printed the directions for you and your mom."

A woman could fall in love with a guy like him. No, that wasn't what Harper meant. Thanks to the lingering effects of the sedative, it was hard to keep her thoughts in focus. *My little boys will be lucky to have him for a father.* That was it.

They returned with a plastic pitcher of red liquid. While Peter filled the cylinder, Harper rocked the glider to prevent her muscles from stiffening. The rapidly cooling air soothed her pleasantly.

"It may take the hummers a day or so to discover this," Peter said as he screwed the base onto the upside-down tube.

Mia gave a hop. "Let's go find some right now."

"And shoo them over like tiny sheep?" Harper teased.

"Oh, Mommy!"

"They don't usually eat at night." Peter righted the tube. "Look—there are feeding stations around the base. Once they figure out that it's here, you might see more than one bird at a time. Hummers have to eat frequently to keep up their energy."

"Do they fight?"

Mia possessed an endless store of questions, and Peter an equally bottomless supply of answers. "They do. But when there's plenty of food, that's less likely. They'll take turns, each hovering at a different height and darting in to get dinner. Oh, I nearly forgot." From the sack, he produced a decal of a hawk and stuck it to the window. "You can peel this off if you don't like it. That's to keep birds from flying into the glass."

"Ouch!" Mia patted the top of her head in empathy.

"You think of everything," Harper said.

"I try." He gave her a tender smile.

She had a question of her own. "How can birds live on sugar and water? Don't they need protein?"

"What's protein?" Mia put in.

"A substance in food that builds our muscles and blood and helps us fight disease," Peter told her.

"I wouldn't have known how to answer that," Harper admitted.

"It's really a long train of amino acids, but I didn't think that would go over well." In the light from the patio fixture, Peter's teeth gleamed. "To answer the first part, hummingbirds eat insects, too. They're useful to have around."

"Better and better," Harper agreed.

Inside, the kitten batted its paw against the screen slider. "You can't come out at night, Po," Mia told the kitten. "And no eating the hummingbirds!"

Looping the feeder over the hook, Peter stepped back to study the height. "I think it's high enough and far enough from the table so Po can't reach it by jumping. But there's no telling how big he'll get, and cats are keen hunters. So keep a lookout."

"You bet." Mia nodded for emphasis. Inside, Po sat on the floor and went to work grooming his fur. "When do the hummers get here?"

"They're probably emailing each other as we speak," Harper teased.

Her daughter ignored the joke. "They *could* show up tonight, couldn't they?" she asked Peter.

"No guarantees, but let's sit out here awhile and watch." After replacing the implements in the tool kit, Peter slid into place next to Harper. When her head tilted and her cheek came to rest on his shoulder, it felt exactly the right height.

Mia frowned. "Does no guarantees mean it might not happen?"

"That's right," he said.

"Oh." The little girl wandered over and was about to climb onto Harper's lap when Peter stretched his arm to block her.

"Your mom's tummy hurts," he said. "How about sitting on my lap instead?" To Harper, he added, "If that's okay."

"It is."

Without hesitation, Mia scrambled into Peter's arms and curled against his chest. Her gaze fixed on the feeder until slowly her lids sank shut.

In the last of the dusk, Harper watched the sky shift into blue-black. Peter's strength surrounded her like a shield, keeping her and Mia safe.

Even without hummingbirds, it was a lovely respite. For this sweet moment, they felt like a family.

Chapter Eleven

The lingering happiness of that special evening with Harper only intensified Peter's longing to have children and begin his new life as a father. By Friday, although busy with work and preparations for his trip, he almost wished he'd accepted the surrogate's invitation to attend the egg transfer.

Several times that afternoon, he phoned Vanessa's husband for updates. A sympathetic man, Tommy Ayres patiently kept Peter in the loop. Dr. Sargent also called afterward with the results. By the time Peter was ready to leave for the airport, he had the good news that three embryos had been implanted and three more were being frozen. The remaining eggs hadn't become fertilized.

"You go enjoy your sister's wedding," Tommy told him after one more call to confirm that Vanessa had arrived home safely and was resting. "My wife already talked to the egg donor. You should have heard them laughing together. They're as excited as kids at Christmas."

"Thank you." *Kids at Christmas.* It was a wonderful image for Peter to hold in his mind as he drove to catch his evening flight.

On the plane, he slept fitfully. The flight lasted just under five hours, and he lost three hours to the time change. Arriving in Baltimore early Saturday, Peter drew on his athletic conditioning to gear up for the day ahead, renting a car to make the hour's drive to the area where his sister lived.

With her usual efficiency, Betty had hired an excellent wedding planner and double-checked the details herself. The outdoor event took place at a manor home that specialized in special occasions. Tents had been set up in case of rain, but although a sprinkling had fallen earlier, the afternoon was sunny and only mildly humid.

Walking down the aisle on her father's arm, Betty was transformed from the tightly wound, too-thin woman Peter had last seen during the winter holidays. At four months of pregnancy, her figure was expanding and her skin glowing. The way her face lit up at the sight of her groom, Greg, waiting at the altar, assured Peter that this was not merely a marriage for the child's sake.

Of course, he mused later as they sat around the head table, he should have realized that his sister, after rejecting motherhood for years, would bring her competitive nature to her new state. Being a mom was the most important job in the world, she informed her family, and little girls—since she was carrying one—were much more fun than little boys.

"Peter may be expecting soon, as well," their father said.

Betty, who'd been informed of the situation, merely smiled, but Greg's stylishly groomed mother, Joan, leaned forward with interest. "I didn't realize you were married."

"I'm widowed."

She blinked, taking this in, and quickly moved on, perhaps assuming he had a girlfriend. "Be sure to sign up for the best preschool in your area as soon as the baby's born."

"He's planning to move here next spring," Greg said.

"Then I'll give you a couple of preschool names," Joan said. "I can email you and your fiancée."

"Mom…" Greg began.

"The waiting lists are years long," Joan continued earnestly. "Being an unmarried couple isn't the obstacle it used to be, but you'll make a better impression if you tie the knot first."

Peter searched for a way to avoid embarrassing her. "It's an unusual situation…."

"He's having a baby by a surrogate," Peter's mother said cheerfully.

Joan paused with her mouth open. Then shut it without responding.

"I'm not sure we need to go into this." The discussion felt awkward to Peter, even though these people were now his relatives.

Greg's father, a dark-haired man named Len, leaned back from his plate and folded his arms. "Isn't that risky? What if this surrogate decides to keep it?"

Before Peter could decide how much to reveal, his parents explained that he was also using an egg donor. Their enthusiasm tempered his discomfort at having his personal details thrust into the conversation. Once he moved here, he supposed he'd be seeing a lot of these people, which meant they'd find out, anyway.

New relatives, new surroundings, even different architecture, he reflected, glancing at the Colonial brick manor across the lawn. This would be a stimulating environment for him and his child-to-be. Yet he missed Harper's low-key ranch house, with its porch glider and brilliant blooms out front.

"Aren't you worried about the child's genetic background?" Len ignored the band members setting up their instruments on a pavilion. "This woman's a complete stranger."

"The egg bank posts profiles." Kerry Gladstone had begged Peter to let her have a peek, but he'd resisted.

"People can lie," responded the groom's father.

"I have to admit, Mom, with your interest in genealogy, I'm surprised you're okay with this." Betty held up her hands, palms forward. "Not that I'm objecting, Peter."

Everyone seemed to be staring at him. "Actually, I do…" What was he saying? "Never mind."

"Better finish," his father muttered. "They'll peck you to death until you do."

"No kidding," his mother said. "Spill!"

Oh, why not? "The donor is an acquaintance." Seeing eyes widen and eyebrows rise around the table, Peter elaborated. "It happened that one of the donors is the widow of a man I used to work with. Angela and I knew her casually, and she has a delightful little girl."

"Is she aware that you're the, uh, father-to-be?" asked his new brother-in-law.

Peter nodded.

"What if *she* wants the baby?" Greg's father seemed stuck on that idea. He was, Peter recalled, a lawyer like his son.

"Under California law, she has no parental rights," he said. "Besides, she's happy with the situation."

"You've talked to her?" His mother appeared torn between fascination and concern. "Maybe we should meet her."

"Bad idea," Betty said.

"Very bad," agreed her father-in-law.

"Let's make it happen," Kerry insisted, aiming a commanding stare at her son.

"The surrogate was just implanted yesterday," Peter told her. "There might not even be a baby. Let's hold off, please. And as for meeting the folks, I wouldn't blame Harper if she nixed the whole idea."

"Harper?" his father said. "Nice name."

"Why's she doing this?" Joan asked.

"For the money, obviously," said her husband.

"I've read that egg donors usually have an altruistic motive as well as a financial one," Betty countered.

Oh, great. Now they were putting Harper under a microscope like a lab specimen.

Mercifully, the bandleader interrupted. It was, he announced over the microphone, time for the bride and groom to take a spin on the dance floor.

Faces alight, Betty and Greg arose. Soon they were gliding around the floor set up beneath the tent while the band played their chosen song, "Can I Have This Dance?" It was liltingly romantic.

Angela would have loved being here, Peter reflected. Yet when he imagined himself taking a woman in his arms, he pictured Harper.

Other guests joined in, and then it was father-daughter time. His dad merrily claimed Betty.

As the others left the table, Peter rose, too. "May I have the honor, Mom?"

"You certainly may."

Peter enjoyed the dance so much that he claimed his sister for the next one, while their parents slipped into each other's arms. Last year, they'd celebrated their thirty-fifth wedding anniversary. How wonderful to see them laughing together like newlyweds.

"You look incredible," he told Betty. That wasn't an idle compliment. With her dark blond hair loose around her shoulders instead of drawn tightly into its usual bun, his sister had a new radiance.

"I'm glad we'll have children about the same age." Her

hand rested lightly on Peter's shoulder. "And that you're moving here."

"I only wish Angela could share the experience." A lump rose in his throat.

"You're being very loyal, having children this way." Betty broke off as they navigated around a little boy and girl, dancing together. Both wore earnest expressions as they struggled with the steps.

What fun Mia would have, Peter thought. A father-daughter dance…well, maybe someday, with his child. She'd never be the same as Mia, though.

His thoughts returned to his sister's comment. "What's loyal about it?"

"Any other guy would go out and find a new wife," she said.

"Angela isn't replaceable," Peter said. "We were a perfect match."

"Is there such a thing?" his sister murmured. "I mean, everybody has their differences."

"I can't recall us arguing."

"Of course not." She made a wry face. "You always gave her whatever she wanted."

Peter shook his head. "That's not true."

Betty winked at her maid of honor, who was dancing with the best man, before returning her focus to him. "I recall that before your wedding, she scratched a couple of your old friends from the guest list."

"My wrestling teammates?" Peter had forgotten about that. "They tended to get rowdy when they'd been drinking. I'd outgrown them, anyway."

"A fact you didn't realize until Angela pointed it out." Betty regarded him fondly. "I'm not criticizing her. I'm just surprised you don't recognize that she had an iron fist in a velvet glove. She certainly ruled the roost."

"Quite the opposite—she waited on me." Peter had felt loved and cherished, not bossed around. "Cooking dinner every night, even though we were both working."

"That she did." His sister came to a halt as the dance segued into something faster. "The relationship suited you both, and that's what counts. Now let's go sit down. I'm past the worst morning sickness, but the baby does like to remind me of its presence."

Betty was wrong about Angela. However, he had no desire to argue.

As he escorted her through the tent to their table, Peter wondered how Harper was feeling. He'd seen her briefly at sports camp during the week, but had missed her yesterday. She must have picked up Mia while he was on a call with Vanessa's husband.

By now, he was sure she'd recovered from her procedure. She and Mia might have spent the afternoon at the beach or a park, taking photos. This evening, they'd bake brownies and read or watch videos.

What a cozy, domestic scene. He could hardly wait to get back.

THE MUSIC POUNDED SO loud Harper's head ached. She steadied her nerves with another sip of her Blue Hawaiian, which tasted of rum, pineapple juice and other delicious things. She confined herself to one drink on outings like this, since she was driving. With this concoction, one round would definitely be enough to relax her.

"I'm glad we're doing this," her neighbor Caroline Carter shouted over the music. The vivacious young woman wore a Hawaiian-style wrap dress befitting the theme of the Suncrest Saloon. A white flower tucked in her shoulder-length hair brought out her beautiful milk-chocolate complexion.

"Me, too," Harper said. "Thanks for suggesting it."

The third woman at their table, Zora Raditch, poked at her drink with a straw. Caroline had proposed the evening as a way to get both Harper and the ultrasound tech back into the swing of dating.

Since Mia had a sleepover at Fiona's place, Harper had agreed. Despite her lack of interest in a serious relationship, she needed to meet men. She'd grown too accustomed to hanging out with Peter for her own good—and for Mia's.

Right now, his family was no doubt introducing him to his sister's friends. The maid of honor and all those bridesmaids—Harper had no idea how big the wedding was—must be swarming over this handsome new guy. By the time he moved to the area, he'd have a little black book full of phone numbers.

A tap on her shoulder drew her attention to a man who bore a slight resemblance to Peter. He appeared a few years older, and his blond hair was thinning at the temples, but her mood lifted. When he nodded toward the dance floor, Harper ignored her annoyance at his lack of manners—couldn't he ask politely?—and uncoiled from her seat.

"You go, girl!" Caroline said, and turned to greet a good-looking fellow heading her way.

"Have fun," Zora mouthed to Harper.

They exchanged sympathetic glances. Both had lost husbands, in very different ways. Harper wasn't sure which was worse: the death of a good man, or a betrayal that undermined Zora's confidence and ability to love again. Now, if a man cheated on you and then died, that might not be so bad.

Half a Blue Hawaiian, and she was already coming up with stuff like that? She'd better quit drinking entirely.

The rhythm of the music took over, and Harper threw

herself into the pure fun of dancing. Her partner's habit of glancing at her breasts took some of the edge off, though.

"I'm Rocky!" he called.

Was that really his name, or one he'd invented for the evening? Harper sneaked a glance at his left hand, but in the dim light she couldn't tell whether he had a wedding ring tan line. Too bad it wasn't acceptable to demand he present photo ID.

"Harper." If she made something up, that could lead to an embarrassing situation with her girlfriends. On second thought, if he addressed her as Desirée or Lolita, they'd get the joke. Well, too late.

The music intensified to an even faster pace, and for a while Harper simply enjoyed herself. She ignored the guy, who was trying too hard, throwing in what he apparently intended as sexy moves that came across as middle-aged and cheesy. Still, not all nice guys were good dancers.

Nice guys didn't lie about their names. But it *might* be Rocky.

"What do you do?" he shouted over the music.

"I'm a nurse." Now, any chance he'd reply with the truth? "What do you—"

He gave her a wolfish grin. "Want to play doctor?"

"No!" Without a backward glance, Harper marched off the dance floor. Seriously, didn't the man have any idea how he came across?

"Loser?" Zora asked when Harper sat down. Caroline was visible through the crowd of dancers, shaking up a storm.

"And then some."

A deep-down longing swept Harper to be held in Peter's arms, to bury her nose in his hair, to move her body against his. She loathed the prospect of meeting anyone else and struggling through another awkward conversation, even if the guy wasn't so obviously a jerk. With Peter, words tripped over one another. He had interesting ideas and facts to share, and a dry sense of humor.

Resting her chin on her hand, Harper thought about the baby or babies they might have created. Vanessa had called her about yesterday's implantation, which was kind of her. What if those two little boys were already growing?

How wonderful to see Peter's intelligence and vitality in a child, and to watch the love on his face as he rocked a baby. She yearned to be there beside him, touching his cheek, sharing his happiness.

I'm falling in love with him.

Stunned, Harper knocked her hand into her drink. Half full, it sloshed a few drops before she caught it.

A waitress appeared as if by magic. "How about a refill?"

"No, thanks." Harper set the glass aside. "I'm done, anyway."

Zora eyed her sympathetically. "Not in a party mood, either?"

"Guess not." Harper was pleased when Caroline returned. "Would you mind if I left?"

"Good timing." Her friend angled her foot to reveal a broken high heel. "I'd dance barefoot, but in this crowd someone's likely to step on me."

The three of them paid and left. As she drove home, Harper wished she had an idea of what to do next about Peter. Mia, the book, the eggs…she'd allowed their lives to become intertwined far more than she should have.

Next weekend, she'd better tell him how she felt. Then he'd understand why she had to stop seeing him.

Chapter Twelve

All week, Harper fought her churning emotions. Despite her efforts, she could tell she came across as grumpy and distracted. Fortunately, everyone at work attributed that to suspense about the surrogate's possible pregnancy, while Mia was preoccupied with the last week at sports camp.

Would she suffer from withdrawal when she no longer saw Peter there or at home? Tough as this situation might be on Harper, she worried more about her daughter's emotions.

"I must be really stupid," she told Stacy over lunch at the cafeteria the following Friday. "How could I let this happen?"

They'd chosen a table on the patio. The August heat had driven other diners indoors, and Harper was grateful for her friend's willingness to sit out here where they could talk privately. And sweat.

"You don't *let* something like this happen," Stacy said, her sprinkling of freckles more pronounced than usual. That was a common side effect of pregnancy, and of summer, too. "It just does."

Harper cracked a rare smile. "I guess I am being tough on myself."

"As usual," Stacy replied over a forkful of salad. Despite the flattering empire waistline of the gown she'd chosen, the bride was trying to keep her weight from ballooning before her big day.

"I'm glad we have the party to look forward to." The combined wedding-baby shower, which Harper and Adrienne were cohosting, was the next event on their schedule. "Mia's helping us plan the refreshments. I had to say no to carrot cake, though. She finds it hard to believe not everyone shares her tastes."

"You guys are a lifesaver. All the same, it's lucky my parents are arriving tonight." They were making the twelve-hour drive from Utah in one day. "I need my mom right now."

"I wish my mother was still alive. For Mia's sake as much as mine." Harper missed having family around. It didn't help that her brother was a no-show.

After Mia's birthday, Harper had sent him a copy of the little girl's book about Po, in an attempt to renew contact in case her brother was suffering from one of his bouts with depression. She'd included a card from them both that said, "We love you." He hadn't responded. With a vacuum in the father figure department, no wonder Mia had taken to Peter so readily.

"Your daughter will be fine," Stacy assured her. "Once school starts, she'll be tied up with friends and activities."

That reminded Harper of some good news. "I requested she be assigned to Paula Humphreys for second grade, and I saw on the school website that we got her." Paula, whose mother-in-law owned the Bear and Doll Boutique, was noted for planning her lessons around her love of animals. Several parents at the hospital had raved about her.

"Congratulations," Stacy said. "Problem solved."

Harper hoped so. She'd purposely kept her encounters with Peter brief this week, and planned another hit-and-run when she picked up Mia tonight. She still hadn't decided how to handle their meeting tomorrow.

That afternoon, a full patient load kept Harper on the run. Then Nora had to race to the hospital to perform an emergency C-section. Harper did her best to postpone the remaining appointments, but a few patients couldn't change their plans. As a result, Nora played catch-up on her return, which meant staying late for both her and Harper.

Harper couldn't ask Stacy to pick up Mia, not with her parents due in town. Since Adrienne worked Friday nights, she was tied up.

Reluctantly, she punched in Peter's cell number. When he answered, his warm greeting shivered through her. *Keep your mind on business.* "I have to work late and I'm trying to find someone to pick up Mia," Harper told him. "There may be a slight delay. I'm sorry. I know it's the last day of camp, and you must have a lot to do."

"No problem." He sounded relaxed. "Why don't I take her to dinner? What time will you be home?"

"Around seven," Harper said. "But I can't ask that."

"It's no trouble. I have to eat, anyway."

Her instincts warned her to argue, but what were the options? "That would be wonderful."

"I have to make a stop on the way but it won't take long," he added. "If that's okay."

"Yes, of course." She nearly offered to pay him back for the meal, but then he'd argue. She'd already kept a patient waiting too long. "Thank you."

"I'll enjoy it," he said.

So would Mia, Harper reflected as she clicked off. Possibly too much.

PERHAPS HE SHOULD HAVE indicated the nature of his errand, Peter reflected as he pulled out of the community college parking lot. Beside him, strapped into her seat, Mia gazed eagerly out of his van.

"Can we go to Salads and More?" she asked. "I like the More part best."

"I do, too." The cafeteria style, all-you-can-eat restaurant, which also served pasta, muffins and other goodies, lay about a mile up the road, beyond the cemetery. Which was where Peter had to stop.

The brass vase on Angela's headstone had been damaged, and the manager had asked him to approve a replacement. In light of the man's impatience to complete the paperwork, Peter had agreed to stop by as quickly as possible.

"We had two hummingbirds this morning," the girl said. "They were squeaking while they ate. I didn't know they did that."

"Some of them do." Peter described how the little birds also created a shrill sound by spreading their tail feathers while diving at high speed. "The males put on an aerial display to impress the females. Plus, they dive-bomb predators that get too close to their nests."

"Doesn't it hurt them?" Mia asked.

"Making the noise? I doubt it."

"Dive-bombing," she amended. "What do they drop, exactly?"

He nearly blurted the first thing that came to mind, but that was hardly accurate, or discreet. "They bomb with their own little bodies, but they don't hurt anyone because they don't hit."

"Cool."

He stopped near the cemetery's main building. "Let's go inside. I have to sign something."

"Okay."

Before they could get out, however, Peter spotted the

manager on the front walkway, talking to a middle-aged couple. The man waved and, excusing himself, strode to the van.

"I'd appreciate it if you'd drive over and take a look, Mr. Gladstone," he said. "I'll leave the paper on the front desk."

"It's installed?" Peter hadn't expected that.

"We had a funeral today and a damaged vase doesn't look good," came the rejoinder. "I'm sure you'll like it."

Peter wasn't certain how Harper would feel about her daughter touring a graveyard. An impressionable youngster might have nightmares. However, Angela's grave lay only a short distance from the driveway, so there was no reason for Mia to get out of the van. "Okay."

With a nod, the manager returned to his clients. Peter put the van into gear.

"They had to replace the vase at my wife's grave," he told Mia.

"What happened to it?"

"I think a lawn mower hit it."

As the van rolled through the green expanse, the little girl pressed her nose to the window. "My grandma Harriett's over there." Mia pointed toward the middle of the lawn. "We brought her flowers for Mother's Day."

"That's your mom's mother?"

She nodded. "I don't remember her. I was only two when she died." As they drove farther, she pointed again. "Daddy's over there."

This child had lost a lot of loved ones for someone so young. Peter hoped the visit was more reassuring than troubling. She seemed at ease so far.

"I used to work with your father." Peter had spent after-school hours with Sean and the wrestling team. A dedicated physical education teacher, the man had been energetic and occasionally abrasive, although never abusive. Since his death, the school had hired a series of inexperienced teachers who either quit or had their contracts dropped. He wasn't an easy man to replace.

In a way, Peter regretted that he and Sean hadn't grown close. A friendship might have developed had Peter accepted his invitations to go target shooting and off-roading in the desert. While he'd been tempted, Angela had disliked being left alone on weekends.

It had been during one of those adventures that Sean's vehicle flipped and crushed him. He'd had a friend with him, but even though help had been summoned swiftly, the medics weren't able to save his life.

Peter parked near Angela's grave, leaving room on the driveway for cars to pass. "I'll only be a minute."

"I'm coming!" Mia opened her door so fast, he had to run around the high vehicle to help her down.

"Are you sure you want to see the grave?" he asked as he lifted her little body to the ground.

"Graves are pretty," Mia said. "They have flowers and stuff."

She didn't seem spooked. Despite his misgivings, Peter decided the simplest course was to get this over with quickly.

As they walked between markers, Mia peered at an engraving. "That was an old man. He was born in 1920."

Peter noted that the fellow had died in 1944, during World War II. Not old at all. But pointing that out might make her sad.

Then, with a familiar twist of grief, he reached the flat stone recording Angela's name, birth and death dates, along with "Beloved wife and teacher." The day of her burial, the pastor's words of comfort—which hadn't comforted him at all—had reached Peter dimly as he tried to accept that the woman he loved was gone forever. That she couldn't feel the sunshine, or see the family and friends gathered around. That he'd never laugh with her or sleep curled together again.

To his embarrassment, tears slid from his eyes. Peter wiped them with the back of his other hand.

"Are you crying?" Mia put her small, warm hand in his. "Does this help?"

"Yes." And it did.

"She smelled nice."

"What do you mean?"

"Mrs. Gladstone." She studied the marker. "I just 'member her perfume."

They must have met at a faculty gathering or a wrestling match. "She thought you were adorable."

"She's a real angel now," Mia said. "Do you think she knows Daddy and Grandma?"

"She certainly knew your father when she was alive."

Mia gazed up at him, her face a younger version of Harper's. "You have to come back."

"Come back?"

"Mommy says you're moving," Mia answered. "But you'll still visit your wife, won't you?"

"Yes, of course." Strange that he hadn't thought about that when he decided to go. Maybe he should relocate Angela's body, especially since her family lived in Virginia. Yet this was supposed to be her final resting place.

And what was he going to do with her china collection? Peter wondered suddenly. He'd rather not ship those cabinets and collectibles to his new home. Maybe he should sell them and donate the money to charity. But that seemed disloyal.

I'm not leaving you behind, honey. I'll still visit when I can.

He imagined he could feel her disapproval. Maybe he

should have her body relocated. Not something to worry about yet, however.

His attention turned to the new vase, which was, after all, the reason for this trip. It bore a simple leaf impression instead of the elaborate floral engraving of the original, which Angela had commissioned during her final illness. On the phone, the manager had explained that he hadn't been able to match the custom design. With a silent apology to his wife, Peter decided to accept it.

"Will you bring my little brother to see me?" Mia asked. "I want to play with him."

"I'll do my best." Gently, Peter released her hand. "We should go eat."

"He'll like the hummingbirds," she said as they walked. "Hey! You can give him a feeder, too."

"That's a good idea." He'd install one as soon as he bought a new house, Peter decided, as a reminder of a special evening.

WHEN HARPER OPENED HER door, Peter noticed strain lines around her eyes. What a long day she'd worked. He'd like to give her a shoulder rub, and they could sit on the porch again and talk about all the things she'd been doing these past two weeks. "How're you feeling?"

"I'm fine." She absorbed the impact of Mia's enthusiastic embrace. "Have a good time, sweetie?"

"We went to see Daddy and Angela!"

So much for introducing the subject gently. "I had to check out a replacement vase at the cemetery. That was the errand I mentioned."

Harper angled aside to let her daughter pass. "I'm afraid we'll have to postpone our meeting tomorrow. Adrienne has to work an extra shift, and I'm watching Reggie. But on Sunday she'll be taking both kids, so let's meet at the

Fullerton Arboretum. The unusual plants should attract some different types of insects." The gardens lay a half-hour drive north.

"Good idea." Peter swallowed his disappointment at the delay. "I'll pick you up."

"Thanks, but I'd like to do some shopping in the area." Her gaze flicked across his, avoiding contact. "Two o'clock at the front entrance?"

"Sure." Was she pushing him away because she was tired, or had he offended her? "I didn't mean for Mia to see the graves. I thought I'd just be running into the main building."

"Did she act upset?"

"I'm the one who needed consoling," he admitted.

"I'll talk to her." Harper shrugged. "It's better to face her feelings, anyway."

"You're not angry?"

Her expression softened. "No. I appreciate your help tonight. It's hard, being a single parent."

"I guess I'll find out." At their feet, a black-and-white face poked out. Seeing the kitten's muscles bunch, Peter bent down to thwart a dash for freedom. "No escape for you, Po."

Tiny claws pricked his hands as he lifted the little creature. They didn't penetrate the skin, a sign that the kitten was displaying annoyance rather than attacking.

"Good catch. I didn't see him." Harper reached for the furry creature. As her arm brushed Peter's, her sweet fragrance stirred his longing. Impulsively, Peter brushed a kiss across her temple.

Harper stepped back, her eyes wide, her breathing rapid. "Why…?"

"I shouldn't have…"

"Mommy! I can't find Po." Mia's voice rang out behind her.

"Right here." Her forehead furrowed, Harper turned away. "Thanks again for watching her."

"My pleasure. Look, if you aren't too tired…" he began.

"I'm afraid I am. You must be worn-out, too." Despite the apologetic words, she seemed to be retreating. "Good night."

"Night." As the door closed, Peter wished he understood her reaction. She hadn't seemed upset with him, but had been far from welcoming.

He was glad they'd have time alone on Sunday. Not entirely alone—they'd be surrounded by other visitors—but without Mia, they might have a chance to restore their relationship to an even footing.

He'd been foolish to yield to his impulse, Peter mused as he went down the walk. By kissing her, even on the temple, he'd violated their arrangement. Harper had donated eggs despite his deceptive behavior. On his behalf and for the baby, she'd taken hormones that messed up her system and had undergone a painful procedure. Caught up in the fertility process and enjoying her companionship, he'd reacted as if they were dating. But they weren't. They'd agreed on that.

On Sunday, they'd straighten this out. Surely Harper shared his belief that these next few months were meant to be treasured. He'd reassure her that he meant to keep his distance, as agreed. Then they could relax and simply have fun.

His spirits rising, Peter could hardly wait until Sunday.

Chapter Thirteen

That evening, Harper and Mia watched a video from one of their last days with Sean. Mia had asked to see it.

Harper's thoughts kept straying to Peter. Why had he kissed her hair? It might simply be a sign of affection, but she sensed there was more.

Could he be developing feelings for her, too?

She rehearsed ways to tell him how she felt without pushing him away. Perhaps something along the lines of "I have to stop spending time with you because I'm starting to care too much." That would give him an opening, in case he felt the same.

Was he ready to let go of his wife? If so, was *she* ready to take their relationship to a new level?

The answer was a slightly nervous yes.

On the screen, she watched her late husband pretend-tussle with his toddler daughter in front of their old house. Mia squealed in delight as he lifted her high. "More, Daddy! More!"

He tossed her up and she spread her arms. "I can fly!"

From behind the camera came Harper's voice. "Sean! Be careful!"

He caught his daughter easily. "Never fear. My little girl can fly. You heard her."

On the couch, Mia cuddled closer to Harper. "Could he still throw me in the air? I'm bigger now."

"Sure. He was a wrestling coach." Watching Sean's muscular body, Harper remembered her husband's strength when he held her. And when they made love…best not to think about how much she missed that. "He could have thrown *me* in the air."

"Really?"

"Well, almost."

The video ended with Sean carrying a squealing, laughing Mia into the house. When the TV went dark, they sat for a moment.

Mia broke the silence. "Thank you, Mommy."

"You're welcome." Although this afternoon's excursion didn't appear to trouble Mia, Harper decided to sound out her daughter. "Did you feel okay about visiting the cemetery today?"

"It was fun."

"Not scary?" she asked as she retrieved the DVD from its tray.

Her daughter shook her head. "Peter's wife is an angel now. He was crying, but I held his hand and he stopped."

Crying, even after two years. Harper's chest squeezed. True, sometimes in the night, she shed a few tears for Sean. But to weep in front of a child…clearly, Peter wasn't ready to move on.

Thank goodness she hadn't blundered into telling him her feelings. She'd have embarrassed them both.

"Good for you," she told her daughter. "That was kind."

"I wish we had Daddy back."

"Me, too."

As she sent Mia to get ready for bed, Harper shivered at how close she'd come to making a fool of herself. How awkward to admit she was falling in love with a man whose heart belonged to his late wife.

She'd better think carefully about what to tell him on Sunday.

PETER HADN'T EXPECTED to find the arboretum parking lot nearly full on a cloudy day when monsoonal moisture turned the air damp. But he was glad Harper had suggested meeting here. It was no wonder the gardens adjacent to California State University, Fullerton, teemed with visitors, considering the wealth of plants and activities. Signs announced classes in everything from yoga to composting to bird-watching for kids.

He ought to organize a field trip for his students, Peter reflected, especially since this was the last year he'd be teaching in the area. While these gardens didn't compare to the U.S. National Arboretum in Washington, D.C., he liked the intimacy here.

Near the entrance, sunlight reflected off Harper's camera lens. In contrast to the rumpled visitors wandering by in loose T-shirts and flip-flops, she seemed coolly composed in tailored shorts and a halter top tied beneath her breasts to reveal a slender waist. Peter felt his body quickening, and hoped she didn't notice. Instead, he hurried to pay the modest admission fee.

"It's my treat," Harper protested, appearing beside him. "I proposed this."

"He-men like me are supposed to pay," he teased.

That brought an ironic smile. "Does that mean you have to carry me over the puddles?"

"No danger of puddles," he responded cheerfully. "I'm sure the arboretum never overwaters."

"Good, because I'd give you a hernia."

"Oh, in your case, I'd use a fireman's carry," he said.

A poke in the ribs greeted this remark. Without waiting for his response, she turned away and aimed her camera at a flower. Or so he thought, until he zeroed in on her subject: a yellow butterfly with black edging and other distinctive markings.

"How did you spot that?" he asked. "It's camouflaged amid all the flowers."

"Photographer's eye." Harper knelt to get a better angle.

Peter waited, content to view the passersby. A couple of children skipped along, chattering gaily. A young woman with Down syndrome spread her arms, luxuriating in the joy of the moment until her parents tugged her along. A group that he guessed were Japanese tourists paused to listen to their guide, and then followed her inside.

After the butterfly took its leave, he and Harper studied a map of the grounds. They decided to head for the primitive plants section in the woodlands garden. "Plants from the Jurassic period," Harper said as they navigated the path. "How fascinating."

"If we're lucky, we'll spot a few dinosaurs lurking about," Peter said.

"Can dinosaurs lurk?" Harper peered skyward, as if a brontosaurus—or, more accurately, an apatosaurus— might appear. "If there are any, I'm sure they'd loom."

"There were small dinosaurs, too," he observed. "And— more appropriate to our subject—giant insects."

Harper wrinkled her nose. "Too big to step on?"

"Depends on your shoe size," Peter said. "Chinese scientists have found fossils of flealike creatures ten times the size of modern fleas. They had large claws and a proboscis like a hypodermic needle."

She shuddered. "How do you know this stuff?"

"Internet," he said. "I had all day yesterday to prepare."

They reached the primitive plants area, thick with ferns. "For the book?"

"And to impress you," he conceded.

Instead of the warm reaction he'd hoped for, Harper trained her gaze on a magnolia, which scientists believed had been one of the earliest flowering plants on earth. "As long as we're discussing the book…"

"Hold on." First, Peter wanted to address something that had been bothering him. "I'm sorry if I behaved inappropriately the other night."

"Mia's fine." To his puzzled look, she explained, "Visiting the cemetery was good for her. She requested a video of Sean, and that's the first time she's done that."

"Glad to hear it." That wasn't his point, though. "About the kiss. I realized I may have given you the wrong impression. We agreed to be friends, and that's how I'd like to keep things."

Harper tensed. "That may not be possible."

"Why not?" He'd assumed that, once he cleared the air, she'd have no reason to distance herself.

She took a deep breath. "Peter, I'm getting too attached to the idea of those babies. This is too hard for me."

That was the problem? "It's the first you've mentioned it."

"I know and I apologize." Her eyes meeting his at last, Harper rushed on. "I keep wanting to hold them and thinking about what they'll be like as they grow. I can't seem to let go emotionally. It's best if I stop seeing you."

A cold chill ran through Peter. He'd looked forward to sharing this pregnancy with her, and her daughter. It felt as if she were casting him into some outer darkness. "Mia asked if I'd bring the babies to visit later, and I said I would."

"You shouldn't have," Harper responded sharply. "She's starting to feel like they're part of our family."

Angela would never have pushed him away like this, Peter thought. She'd have taken his hands in hers, gently explained what mattered and guided him to her point of view. But he didn't want to think about Angela at the moment. He wanted go on being friends with Harper.

Only he didn't know how to make his point without sounding as if...well, as if he were offering more emotional involvement than he was capable of. And more, evidently, than Harper was willing to accept.

"Let's work on the book by email from now on," she said. "We've settled the important decisions about it, anyway."

Peter stepped aside to make room for a man in a wheelchair and his companion. When they'd gone on, he said, "Let's think this over and talk again. There has to be a better way to handle it."

"Email will be fine," she said stubbornly.

"Not just about the book."

"Then what?"

There was more going on than she'd told him, Peter sensed, but he had no idea what. Before he could pull his thoughts together, his phone rang.

The name Tom Ayres leaped out at him. Why was Vanessa's husband calling him?

"I'd better take this," he said.

HARPER WASN'T SURE WHAT she'd expected from Peter. Since he'd made it plain he had no personal interest in her, why was he arguing about completing the book by email?

She forgot all that as she listened to his side of the conversation. "Is she sure?...Isn't it too early?" He looked stricken.

By the time he clicked off, a hard knot inside warned of what was coming. Ten days since the egg transfer. Vanessa's period must have started.

Peter planted his hands on his hips, chest heaving as if he'd run a race. When he straightened, his face was pale.

"No babies," Harper guessed.

A nod. "We should go." Without waiting for an answer, he started back along the path.

She hurried in his wake. Rationally, they'd both known the odds of achieving a pregnancy on the first try were no better than one in three. And Vanessa could try again with the frozen embryos. But this hurt, and if it bothered her, it must be even worse for him.

Harper might have tried to comfort Peter, but the timing was terrible. From the set of his shoulders and length of his stride, he seemed angry.

In the parking lot, he finally halted and let her catch up. "This is hard to deal with." The moisture in his eyes showed *how* hard. "The baby became real to me. I didn't realize how much."

A dark sense of loss filled Harper, as well. "Me, too. Not the same way, but…"

"But, as you said, you were growing too attached."

To him, also. She hadn't realized how much she'd longed to see him with a baby in his arms. Their baby, or his baby—she couldn't think straight, so she deflected. "It's going to be difficult breaking the news to Mia."

"We shouldn't have built up her expectations."

"I tried not to, but…" She'd tried not to do a lot of things, Harper thought regretfully. "Vanessa will try again, won't she?"

"Yes." He paused, his expression masked. "We'll use the frozen embryos. If that doesn't do it, I can't ask you to go through this process again."

Harper had to admit, she wasn't sure she could bear it. "Peter, I'm sorry."

"You were right about using email." His frayed voice showed how hard he was struggling to speak calmly. "I hope Mia won't feel that I'm abandoning her."

"She knows you're moving, anyway." Harper longed to touch his cheek. They ought to share their sorrow and renew their hope together.

That was what couples did. But they weren't a couple.

"The next time will succeed," she said. "I suppose it's naive to believe in my dream, but I do."

"Send me the photos you took today and I'll fit them into the text," Peter said.

"Will do."

"See you." Jaw clenched, he walked to his van.

Losing these babies—embryos, Harper reminded herself—had hit him hard. But the loss only underscored how far apart they were, and always would be.

As she slid behind the driver's wheel, she blinked back a sheen of tears. Those little boys…maybe they weren't meant to be. Or maybe she'd have to wait until she found another man to love. A man whose heart wasn't forever committed to someone else.

She'd intended to go on a journey of discovery with this donation. It wasn't turning out to be the journey she'd envisioned.

"I NEARLY SAVED A WHITEFLY for you." Adrienne made a face. "But, Harper, friendship only goes so far."

"Very funny."

"Seriously, I do like to help."

"You've done more than your share." Harper had captured several interesting insects in her friend's vegetable garden over the past month or so. It was fortunate she'd racked up so many images, because in the week since she and Peter parted ways, she'd found it almost impossible to pick up her camera.

She'd brought it to Adrienne's house today, but only to document the wedding/baby shower. They'd decked out the family room with white wedding bells and blue-and-pink baby cutouts, and set out refreshments: a fruit tray, vegetables and dip, cakes and cookies and a table of party favors.

Through a rear window, Harper watched Reggie and Mia romping in the large yard. The little girl had insisted on wearing the same sunny yellow dress she'd put on for church. Although it was likely to be ruined by the time the guests arrived, Harper didn't care. She was glad to see her daughter enjoying herself.

It had been a rough week, with both of them down in the dumps. Mia had cried when she learned there wouldn't be any babies this time, and she kept asking for Peter. When told he had to prepare for the start of school, she'd responded that she had to do that, too, which to her meant reading picture books aloud to Po. The one Peter had given her was the favorite.

Today, as Harper helped set up for the party, she yearned to unload her feelings, which still felt raw. But although she and Adrienne were friends, they'd never shared the kind of intimacy she'd had with Vicki. That was partly because, while growing up, Harper had been in awe of the older, highly focused Adrienne, and that hadn't changed in later years when she became an obstetrician.

Even after Adrienne moved into this family home three years ago, providing stability to Reggie as Vicki's bipolar disorder worsened, she'd remained an intimidating figure. Then, grief at Vicki's death had brought them together these past eight months, along with the need to support each other as single parents.

Now, with nearly an hour to spare, they were relaxing in the family room. "How's the picture book progressing?" Adrienne smoothed her blond hair, which she'd pulled back with a jeweled clip.

"I'm nearly finished with the photos, unless he thinks of anything we're lacking." Harper fingered her camera case.

"What's going on between you two, anyway?"

"You mean me and Peter?"

"Is there anyone else?"

"No, but…" Harper nearly shrugged off the topic. Oh, who was she kidding? Adrienne had seen how they interacted at the birthday party, and probably received an earful from Mia. "We were getting too close."

"Too close for whom?"

"For him. And me." She sighed. "We were great pals— until I fell for him."

"You're sure he doesn't feel the same way?" her friend probed.

"There's only room in his heart for one woman, and that's Angela." Harper explained about him weeping over his wife's grave. "To him, anything beyond friendship is out of the question. I was more vulnerable than I'd expected, so I broke it off. Not that there was much to break off, except in my imagination."

"Sounds like you miss him." Adrienne shifted her perch on a well-worn sofa that had been freshened with lacy pillows. Above her, a montage showed photos of her parents, of her and Vicki growing up and of Reggie as an infant.

None included his father, whom Harper only vaguely recalled meeting when he and Vicki were dating. He'd left town soon after his son's birth and never so much as sent a dime to help his son. Although she and Stacy had urged Vicki to sue for child support, she'd refused.

Peter was nothing like that. If he were, she wouldn't hurt

so intensely. All week, she'd felt as if someone had yanked a rug from beneath her feet. Vanessa's failure to conceive had contributed to her moodiness, but also to her concern for how Peter might be reacting to the loss.

"Any words of advice?" Harper asked.

"About what?"

"Getting over him," she said. "I don't know much about relationships. It's not as if I dated much before I got married. Sean was the only man I ever cared about."

"What makes you think I know anything about relationships?" Adrienne asked.

"Well, you're a doctor," Harper noted. "And older." During their teen years, when the five-year age gap seemed enormous, Adrienne had been a font of information about boys.

"I've never been married." The other woman stretched. "I was engaged once, but that fell apart."

"Why?" Harper ventured. She didn't mean to be nosy, but she'd opened up about her own problems.

Adrienne shrugged. "It was during my residency. My fiancé was an attending physician who said he didn't care for kids. Then he got one of the nurses pregnant. Suddenly he couldn't wait to marry her and play daddy."

"What a jerk." Harper's heart went out to her friend, who wasn't able to have children. As a teenager, she'd undergone an emergency hysterectomy following a car crash. The driver, her then-boyfriend, had been drunk.

"I've been over it for a long time." Adrienne straightened as a car rolled down the street, stopping nearby. "I'm glad I can be here for Reggie and that I have him. Other than that, I've fantasized about finding the right man, but that's hardly likely, is it?"

"I'm beginning to think men aren't worth the trouble."

"Me, too." Glancing at a cutout set of wedding bells

adorning the refreshment table, Adrienne chuckled. "Thank goodness it's worked out better for Stacy. That's probably her and her mom now."

Outside, Harper heard familiar voices, and then the bell rang. Time to break out the party favors and silly games. And to wonder why she, despite having had a happy marriage to Sean, had reached the same conclusion about men as Adrienne.

Chapter Fourteen

Bad luck comes in threes.

Peter didn't believe in superstitions, but Angela had. Once, after a fender-bender parking lot accident was followed by a twisted ankle at home, she'd deliberately broken a teacup in hopes of forestalling a third mishap. He couldn't recall now whether it had worked.

He almost hoped the old saying was true, because if so, by now he was due for some good luck, he reflected as he parked outside his parents' house on a Saturday morning in late September. As he went to the door, Peter averted his gaze from the for-sale sign on the lawn. No sense dwelling on how sad he felt about saying goodbye to this beloved home.

He was still reeling from his recent triple dose of bad luck. Harper's withdrawal had hit him harder than he'd expected. The emailed photos only reminded him of how much he longed to be sitting beside her, joking and talking.

The second misfortune had been Vanessa's failure to implant, although there was hope again. This past week, she'd undergone a transfer of the remaining three embryos. As hard as Peter tried not to dwell on what might be happening inside her, fear and longing battled through his heart. This was the last chance with Harper's eggs. If it didn't work, then what?

Yet he'd had little time to dwell on that, thanks to his third stroke of bad luck. And how was he going to tell his parents about that?

When he rang the bell, his mother opened it so fast, she must have been watching out the window. "Hi, sweetie!" Kerry gave him a hug. "I don't know how we let a whole month go by." They hadn't met since his sister's wedding, although they'd talked on the phone.

"It's not like we aren't in touch."

"There's no substitute for personal contact." His dad gave him a clap on the shoulder.

Peter rubbed his arm, feigning pain. "Mercifully." Why were both parents waiting at the door? Eager for word of the babies? "It's too soon for news from Vanessa."

"We're keeping our fingers crossed." His mom led the way into the dining room. Tablecloth, flowers, holiday china. She'd set a fancy table for a simple brunch.

"This is beautiful," Peter told her. "What's the occasion?"

"Having you over is always an occasion," she said, a little too brightly.

"Mom?"

"Food's ready." She ducked into the kitchen.

The aroma of bacon was soon joined by the irresistible sight of pancakes and scrambled eggs. "What a feast." Peter appreciated all this work. He was the one who'd requested that they eat early, since he planned to attend Cole's wedding that afternoon.

"We've been reading about some belt-tightening in your school district," Rod said as they passed the serving plates. "I hope that hasn't affected you."

Suddenly, the food didn't look as appetizing. "I'm afraid it has."

"They can't lay you off." Kerry paused with her fork

in midair. "The district has to notify you the previous spring if that's a possibility." Preliminary layoff notices— usually more than necessary, just in case—had to be sent by March. Budgets were firmed up in May, except when the legislature kept changing its allocations…like this year.

"My job's safe, in a sense." Peter had enough seniority to survive the cuts. But not enough to keep his favorite classroom. "However, the principal has reassigned me to teach physical education."

His parents sat stunned. They knew how much he loved biology. Even though he had his P.E. credentials, that had always been a secondary field for him.

"When?" Rod asked.

"I got the news two weeks after classes started. What a mess." Peter took a swallow of orange juice before continuing. "The state cut funding, the high school dropped its Japanese language program and that teacher had seniority over me."

"And a biology credential, I assume," his father muttered. "I hope he or she has kept up-to-date."

"She's been teaching one freshman biology class," Peter confirmed. "But she doesn't especially like the subject. How she's going to do a full slate of the classes, including Advanced Placement, I have no idea."

"Meanwhile, you're running around like crazy figuring out new lesson plans," Kerry summed up.

Peter appreciated that, as retired teachers, his parents understood what he had to deal with. Maybe it was fortunate that, thanks to them, he had only this year before his departure for Maryland. Yet he regretted not being able to put in more time with some of the students he'd been mentoring. The outstanding kids would adjust well; they had their inner drive and usually support at home. His concern was for a group of struggling kids who, last year, had begun to blossom with his encouragement and extra tutoring sessions.

He hated leaving them. He'd been counting on having at least one more year to bring out their potential.

"You must be frustrated," his father said.

"And exhausted," Peter admitted. "On the positive side, I put together a proposal for the picture book and sent it to a couple of agents." When he ran out of patience with lesson plans, he'd found the project a welcome relief. And he felt closer to Harper when he was writing it. "Maybe I can have a second career earning—what do children's book authors make? A few thousand bucks a year?"

"But I'll bet it's fun," his mother said.

"There's that." He returned his attention to the meal. No sense letting his other problems spoil his appetite. "You've outdone yourself, Mom."

"Just something I whipped up."

"Right." He grinned.

After they'd cleaned their plates and his father had served the coffee, Kerry gave a little cough. It sounded like a signal to his dad. Now what? With so much on his mind, Peter had forgotten his earlier impression that his parents were hiding something.

It reminded him of the evening they'd revealed his sister's pregnancy. Now what?

His father spoke up. "We have a little news."

"It can't be good, or you'd have told me sooner." Peter rested his elbows on the table.

"It's not that bad." His mother's frown lines hinted otherwise.

"We have a strong bid on the house," Rod said. "The sold sign goes up on Monday."

They'd only had the place on the market for a few weeks. "That was fast."

"The agent says we priced it right for the market," his father noted.

"How long…?" He couldn't finish the question.

"Sixty-day escrow." His mother watched him closely.

Then this home would belong to someone else. Peter tried to stay positive. "Have you found a place in Maryland?"

"Not yet." His father went on talking, with his mother adding a detail here and there, as they outlined their plans. Next week, they'd fly there to tour listed properties. If they didn't find a place right away, they'd rent short-term. By Thanksgiving, they'd be gone. It was only a few months sooner than expected. Yet despite his decision to relocate, Peter saw, he hadn't truly prepared emotionally. Now the future was arriving with lightning speed. Should he leave earlier than planned? Betty's mother-in-law had emailed him not only about preschools but also about the private high school her son had attended, where she served on the board. Just last week she'd mentioned that a biology teacher was leaving midyear, due to her husband's job transfer. Peter had set the information aside without paying much attention.

If Vanessa didn't get pregnant, he'd have no reason to stay in California. Even if she did, he could fly in to see her like the French couple had done.

No reason to stay. Peter's gut tightened. No reason except…

He'd see Harper at the wedding today for the first time since they parted company last month. Her quick laughter, her sharp sideways glances, her soft mouth. Would he encounter welcoming warmth, or had she pushed him out of her thoughts as easily as she'd ejected him from her life?

Not easily. That was unfair.

As he took his leave of his parents, Peter didn't know

what he hoped would happen between him and Harper at the wedding. Something to help him make up his mind.

Or maybe a reason to stay.

"PETER'S HERE!" MIA raced into the bride's room, her hair ribbon askew. Harper reached down to straighten it and check her daughter's dress. Despite Mia's running back and forth to the wedding chapel foyer, the little girl looked lovely, if a little out of breath.

"Who's Peter?" asked Ellie. The bride's sister, wearing her blue-and-purple matron-of-honor dress, peered up from the curling iron that she was applying to Stacy's hair. Instead of a veil or a hat, the bride had chosen narrow crisscrossed golden headbands set with pearls and rhinestones, a style that suited her Grecian dress and left most of her hair loose.

"He's, uh…" Mia turned to Harper.

"A friend," she said.

In the mirror, Stacy rolled her eyes.

"More than a friend?" Ellie guessed.

"Long story." Harper surveyed the bride, who was standing up to avoid wrinkling her gown. With her bulge becoming more pronounced every day, Stacy could have passed for a fertility goddess.

"I'm going to sit with him," Mia announced.

"You're going to sit with Adrienne and Reggie, as we arranged," Harper corrected. "Besides, he probably brought a date." She tried to ignore a twinge in her chest.

"He'd better not," Stacy said. "I invited him as your plus-one."

"This is getting more interesting by the minute." Ellie finished her ministrations. "Tell me more."

"I don't know what it said on his invitation. It came from you, not me." Harper was about to remind her daughter again to follow their seating plan, but Mia had already scooted into the hall. "Oh, for heaven's sake!"

"Somebody's got a crush," Ellie said.

"I do not!"

"I meant your daughter." Stacy's sister smirked.

Stacy was fighting a smile, too. Well, never mind what they thought. Never mind what her heart told her, either.

In the wide mirror, Harper studied her reflection. She'd curled her hair, now chin length, into a pageboy. The blue-trimmed lavender dress suited her figure, which had lost the extra pounds she'd put on while taking hormones. As for her cheeks, they were pink from embarrassment.

"You certainly don't need any blusher," Ellie teased.

Harper glared.

"Okay, that expression might work on me if you weren't my kid sister's buddy, but you're out of luck," the other woman announced. "So, is this Peter cute? I hope Mia does sit with him so I can pick him out when we're up front."

"No ogling the guests." Stacy slipped her feet into strappy high-heeled sandals. "Has anybody seen Cole? I can't believe he scheduled surgery this morning." The last operation had been due to end three hours ago, but might have run long. He hadn't stopped in to announce his arrival since, according to tradition, the groom wasn't supposed to see the bride before the ceremony.

"It never occurred to him that cutting people open wasn't appropriate on his wedding day?" Ellie asked.

"Guess you have a few things to learn about your new brother-in-law," Harper said. "And I'm sure he's here. Cole's head over heels in love. He'd never be late."

"I just hope he doesn't lose the ring." Stacy grinned. "Oh, who cares, as long as we both make it to the altar."

"With Dr. Tartikoff as best man, the ring wouldn't dare

disappear." Harper gave a start as someone rapped on the door.

She opened it to admit Stacy's parents, Ellen and Alastair Layne, who strolled in holding hands. After struggling with marital problems, the couple had recently attended a marriage renewal weekend. Since then, according to Stacy, they'd been acting like newlyweds.

"How's it going?" Ellen asked.

The bride's father beamed. "Honey, you look incredible."

Stacy took a deep breath. "Thanks, Dad." She and her father had quarreled after he learned about her unplanned pregnancy, but that was in the past.

Tears pricked Harper's eyes. Pleased as she was for Stacy, she missed her own parents. And having a husband who loved her, someone to hold on to and cherish. A man who, on her mental screen, resembled Peter more than Sean.

This isn't about me. It's Stacy's day, and she deserves the most wonderful wedding in the world. Don't you dare act gloomy.

Under the guidance of the wedding planner, the small group assembled in the empty foyer. Belatedly, Harper wished she'd checked on Mia. No help for that now.

When the processional music began, Harper went first, as they'd rehearsed. Clutching her bouquet, she took measured steps, keeping pace with the music.

Ahead of her, at the altar, Cole fidgeted in anticipation as he gazed past Harper. Beside him, the fertility department chief waited with a confident tilt of the head. Dr. Tartikoff's usual sardonic expression had morphed into an almost goofy grin. As for the other groomsman, Lucky Mendez, whose tux hid his tattoos, he appeared braced to leap to the groom's rescue if needed. Just what Harper would expect from Cole's ever-efficient office nurse.

Vaguely, she noted that the chapel was nearly full. Most of the guests were hospital staff, she presumed. Harper didn't dare sneak sideways glances and risk tripping.

Reaching the altar, she took a position that left space for Ellie. The bride's sister approached gracefully down the aisle.

Now that she had the chance, Harper zeroed in on her daughter and the man beside her. Mia had found a place with Peter, after all.

In a dark suit and gray striped tie, the man took Harper's breath away. Across the rows, he met her gaze with an openness that sent warmth simmering right down to her dyed-to-match blue shoes. Had he longed for her, too? Was she insane even to speculate about that?

He hadn't brought a date, she saw with relief. On his right sat an elderly couple she didn't recognize.

Mia gazed joyfully up at him. *"Someone has a crush."* The remembered comment brought Harper up short.

On Mia's other side, Adrienne gave Harper a resigned shrug. As for Reggie, he wiggled around and knelt backward on his chair as the music shifted into the bridal march. His aunt had to grab the seat back to prevent it from tipping.

Stacy appeared in the entry, aglow with happiness. The chapel seemed to brighten as she stepped forward between her mother, elegant in a golden dress, and her tuxedoed father. Harper's heart lifted, sharing this magical moment. Blinking back tears, she watched the Laynes hand their daughter to Cole.

"I do!" the groom announced, although no one had asked him anything.

Chuckles ran through the crowd.

Stacy squeezed her husband-to-be's arm. "Not yet," she said.

"Soon," the minister assured them, and began the service.

Chapter Fifteen

Another wedding. Another happy couple. Another pregnant bride. Finishing his meal in the banquet hall, Peter was grateful to have been invited, even though Harper and Mia were placed at the head table and he was out in the boondocks. A sense of good fellowship filled him, just as it had at his sister's wedding last month.

Since the people at his table included several hospital staff members along with Una and Jim Barker, who were having twins using the bride's donated eggs, the conversation featured babies, pregnancies and the fertility program.

Peter kept quiet about his personal situation, given the uncertainty regarding Vanessa's possible pregnancy. He'd hate to be asked what he'd do if the eggs failed to implant, because he didn't know.

As the bride and groom claimed their first dance, he tried to picture his wife on their wedding day. What kind of gown had she worn? For heaven's sake, he had a DVD and a keepsake book, not to mention the dress itself preserved in an acid-free display box. He could take them out and look at them anytime. Perhaps he'd do that tonight.

Plenty of people had told him that two years of mourning was enough. That anyone who clung to a deceased spouse for so long must be weak in the head, or morbidly self-indulgent.

Peter shook off the idea. He wasn't clinging to anyone. He had room in his heart for feelings, just not the same kind.

As if on cue, he spotted Harper wending her way to the dance floor on the arm of Cole's male nurse, a muscular fellow with a military-style haircut. As they walked, they didn't sway toward each other, or bend their heads together as if sharing a private word. There was nothing special between them, Peter reflected with relief, and then dismissed his flash of jealousy as unworthy of him, and Harper.

A waving motion caught his eye. At the head table, Mia was signaling him. Peter grinned. What a sweetheart.

About to wave back, he realized she was nodding along with the music. Well, why not?

Excusing himself from his table, Peter went to join her. Catching a curious glance from the matron of honor, he gave her a polite nod before turning to Mia. "Would you care to dance, young lady?"

"I thought you'd never ask!" With that grown-up remark, she jumped to her feet and darted toward the dance floor.

Heaven help the local boys when she reached her teens, Peter thought in amusement. She should have a father to protect her from them, too.

Following a lilting opening song for the bride and groom, the disc jockey shifted to a fast number. Mia gyrated merrily, her blue dress swirling. Peter took her hand and helped her spin, to her delight and that of the guests around them.

He caught Harper's gaze. What a sweet, wistful expression.

The music changed. Time to switch partners. Peter made eye contact with Adrienne at a nearby table, and nodded toward Reggie, who was bouncing in his chair.

She grabbed her nephew, said something in his ear and propelled him in Mia's direction.

"Look who's cutting in," Peter told her, and yielded his spot to the little boy. Jacket rumpled, tie crooked and a spot of food on one cheek, Reggie began to jump about enthusiastically. Although Mia's nose twitched, she didn't object.

Where was Harper?

He saw her dancing with a guy Peter didn't recognize and wished would disappear. Out of courtesy, he waited a few minutes until the tempo slowed, then cut in.

"You look beautiful," he told Harper, taking her in his arms. What inadequate words to describe her vivid expression and the sensual way she glided against him, her heels putting them at almost the same height.

"You should wear a suit more often." Her breath tickled his ear.

Intoxicated by her fragrance, Peter had trouble responding coherently. "To play soccer and coach wrestling?"

"In the shower would be fine, too." Her cheek brushed his, and she stumbled a little as he steered her around another couple.

"Too much champagne?" he murmured.

"Only half a glass," she replied. "I'm driving."

"Not right now, you aren't," he said, and gripped her more firmly around the waist.

Harper yielded readily, her body generating heat against his. For Peter, the room faded until there was no one but the two of them and nothing but their natural, tantalizing connection.

"I've missed you," he murmured.

She caught her breath. "Oh, Peter."

"I…" He broke off as, from the corner of his eye, he saw a painfully familiar figure in a lacy white dress. There was the scooped, beaded bodice he'd forgotten earlier, the ivory skin and slender neck, and Angela's wounded gaze trained on him.

Startled, Peter regarded the woman directly. It was only Stacy, and she didn't appear distressed at all.

"You're acting like you just saw a ghost," Harper said.

He didn't attempt to cover his reaction. "I think I did."

"You mean *that* ghost?" Harper drew back. "I should have expected it."

The music stopped. The deejay invited them all to a corner table, where the bride and groom were about to cut the cake.

Peter caught Harper's arm. "What did you mean, you expected it?"

"Never mind." She withdrew from his grasp.

"We should finish this conversation." A dance floor might not be the best place to discuss sensitive matters, but he hadn't meant to disappoint her. Or to drive her away.

"I think it's finished."

"Harper…" Peter didn't dare say any more, because here came Mia. She'd shed Reggie and acquired a slightly older girl as a companion.

"Can I play laser tag tomorrow with Gloria?" she asked her mom.

Harper responded with a puzzled smile. "Gloria? Oh, you're Ellie's daughter! From Utah."

The matron of honor appeared behind them. "My boys are dying to play, and it's hard on Gloria, being the only girl. Stacy recommended a place near here, and we've set it up for two o'clock. I'd be grateful if you'd let Mia come, and of course you're welcome to join us."

"We *were* planning a trip to the zoo, but that can wait." Harper didn't sound crazy about the idea, Peter noted, but both girls were appealing to her with tented hands and cries of "Please! Please!"

"Laser tag gives me a headache," she told the other woman. "I can bring her over to wherever you're staying or meet you at the game station."

"No need for that. We'll pick her up." There was a hurried exchange of data, while the girls jumped up and down, cheering.

"You come, too!" Mia demanded of Peter, but he begged off.

Harper would be home alone tomorrow afternoon. That struck him as the perfect time to talk uninterrupted.

NOT ALL MEN LET WOMEN down, Harper mused on Sunday as she watched Ellie's SUV pull away from the house. Stacy's sister had apparently found a great husband, and so had Stacy. Their parents had stuck together, too.

If Sean had lived, he and Harper might have enjoyed the same kind of long-term marriage. But he hadn't. And the truth was that, although he'd been more attentive than her own father, he'd spent half of his weekends out in the desert with his buddies and his ATV—which had killed him.

Retrieving her camera, Harper went into the backyard. Earlier, she and Mia had found a tiny eggshell on the patio. If it was from a hummingbird's nest, there might be little hummers flitting about.

As she observed the flowering bushes closest to the patio, she tried in vain to remember any occasion when her father had spent time with her alone. A civil engineer, he'd worked long hours, and then assumed a heavy load of volunteer activities. When she was sixteen, she'd begged him to take her to a father-daughter dance. Apologetically, he'd explained that it conflicted with an important planning commission meeting.

That night, driving home, he'd fallen asleep at the

wheel and crashed. Not only had he left Harper adrift as she struggled through adolescence, he'd stranded the wife who'd depended on him emotionally and financially. And he'd never resolved his testosterone-fueled conflicts with Jake, then eighteen, who'd enlisted in the army soon afterward.

In a way, she'd married a guy a lot like dear old dad. Neither man had chosen to die prematurely, Harper conceded. But if they'd put their family first instead of last among their priorities, they might both be alive.

Now she'd fallen for a man who put the ghost of his late wife ahead of her. *I must be a glutton for punishment.*

A *whoom* drew her attention to her surroundings. That sound indicated a hummer for sure. And there it was, hovering at the feeder, tiny wings a blur as it fed.

Harper had preset the camera to capture high-speed images. Now, she adjusted the focus and lost herself in the pleasure of immortalizing a bird scarcely four inches long. The iridescent deep pink of the throat marked it as male—she'd read up on the subject—while the rest of the feathers shaded between gray and green. The bird showed no alarm as Harper circled, since it had become accustomed to her presence.

In the depths of the house, the doorbell sounded. It was too soon for Mia to return. With a touch of impatience, she switched off the camera's power.

She opened the door to Peter. Unprepared for the surge of joy she felt, Harper stood drinking in his questioning gaze, the dark blue T-shirt stretched across his well-muscled chest and the intoxicating scent of his aftershave lotion.

"What…?" She hadn't received any messages from him.

"I bring good news." He held up a sheet of paper that

appeared to be a printed-out email. "It deserves to be delivered in person."

"When you knew Mia would be gone?" she asked. But, like the sucker she was, she let him in.

Peter shut the door behind him. "I queried an agent. She loves the proposal and the pictures, and wants to represent us. What do you say?"

Harper couldn't believe it. She blurted the first thing that occurred to her. "She replied on a Sunday?"

"I found it in my in-box when I got home last night." As Peter handed it to her, his palm brushed her cheekbone. "Aren't you pleased?"

"I am. And stunned."

"Your photos put us over the top." His mouth drifted toward hers. "She says they're exceptional. As if I didn't already know that."

Harper lost track of what he was saying. She tilted up her face and parted her lips, brushing his and letting the impact glimmer through her. The paper fluttered to the floor, and they left it there.

Her arms circled his neck. With a deep moan, Peter drew her tighter, his hardness arousing her and awakening her.

"We should celebrate," he murmured when they came up for air.

"Champagne." Stacy had insisted Harper take home a bottle left from yesterday's reception, reminding her that a pregnant bride couldn't drink.

"Or something better."

"Or something better," Harper agreed.

Why not? They were both adults.

She slid up his T-shirt, loving the feel of his firm body. When he cupped her bottom and kissed her again, years of restraint melted.

Harper's breathing sped as they stumbled through the house into her bedroom. The room where she'd slept alone far too long.

But not today.

Chapter Sixteen

Peter hadn't realized how much he'd held back when he'd made love to his wife. She'd been delicate, leaving most of the action to him. With Harper, everything was different. *He* was different—more powerful, more passionate, more sensual.

She had an incredible body, sleek and contoured, and she used it like a tigress. Not that his response required any stimulation. They moved in harmony as he caressed her breasts, teased her tongue with his and slipped off her silky lingerie.

Only when they were naked did a glimmer of practicality intervene. "I didn't bring any protection." He hadn't planned for this.

"I have some, just in case." Chestnut hair hid Harper's face as she leaned over to riffle through a drawer in the nightstand. "Lucky thing, huh?"

"Yes." Not that there was much chance of impregnating her, given his medical issues.

She sat on the bed, the box of condoms in her hand. Was she hesitating? Peter propped himself on one elbow, his palm tracing the curve of her waist. "If you're having second thoughts, I'll understand."

"Stop understanding," Harper commanded, and opened the packet.

Pleased, he slid the protection into place. When he finished, she rolled to face him, legs tangling with his, her mouth exploring his neck and the pulse of his throat.

A tigress. Transforming him into a tiger.

The yearning that he'd ignored for too long drove Peter to pin her against the pillows. A long kiss, and he eased inside her, sensation roaring through his body. Her answering gasps urged him onward.

They were soaring, battling, twisting. On top, she plundered him rhythmically, until Peter could barely restrain himself. He wanted to prolong the ecstasy, to keep her entirely his as long as possible, but fireworks exploded, sending him into a frenzy. She arched her back, crying out, her fiery reaction matching his. The joy intensified until he half believed it might last forever, and then brilliant colors filled him, sweeping him over a threshold into bliss.

Chest heaving, body sheened with moisture, Harper settled into the curve of his arm. Peter lay spent, his breathing gradually returning to normal.

"That was some celebration," he said.

"We didn't even crack open the champagne."

"Next time." He hoped there'd be many next times.

They lay curled together for a while before she spoke again. "Peter, I need to have some idea where we stand. For my daughter's sake if nothing else."

Where they stood. Good question. "Harper, we can sort things out," he said.

"Then why do you sound dubious?"

"It's just that my life's gotten complicated."

She sat up, pulling the sheet around her. "Complicated how?"

Wishing they'd had an opportunity to talk before this, he explained about his reassignment at school and about his parents' house selling with a two-month escrow. "I wasn't going to move until next summer…."

"But you've decided to go sooner," she said tightly. "I get it. Hello and goodbye."

"I just found out about their house yesterday." Why was she so irate? This intimacy was new and unexpected. Peter had never been good at thinking on the fly. "Nothing's decided."

"You couldn't have told me about this before we made love?"

He blinked, considering his answer. "The letter from the agent seemed more important."

"And then you were too busy getting me in the sack." Eyes blurry with tears, she swung out of bed.

"That was mutual."

"A nice fling on your way out the door and out of our lives." Face averted, she snatched her clothes from the floor.

"Absolutely not." If only he could grab this conversation like a soccer ball and halt the play. He needed a moment to catch his breath and his train of thought. "Harper, this wasn't calculated. I haven't figured out the next step."

"It's not entirely up to you."

"I didn't mean to imply that it was." On the street, a vehicle braked to a halt. "That can't be Mia already."

"It's sooner than I expected." Harper began pulling on clothes. "Hurry!"

Peter yanked the covers into place and grabbed his pants and underwear. "I'll put them on in the bathroom. We can say we were discussing the book."

"Gee, you think fast when you have to."

"Only when something's obvious." He disliked sarcasm, although he supposed that was how she reacted when someone hurt her. How had he managed to do that?

In the hall, Peter collected his T-shirt and ducked into the bathroom. As he struggled into uncooperative jeans, he kept trying to figure out how they'd gone from tenderness to sword's point in a matter of seconds. Whatever he'd done wrong, it escaped him.

From the living room, he heard Ellie explaining that her overexcited boys had been so aggressive in the laser tag session that the manager had asked them to leave. "It was embarrassing," she said. "I'm sorry your little girl had to witness this."

"I had fun," Mia responded cheerfully. "They were acting mean and they deserved to be punished."

Peter washed his face. When he came up for air, he heard no more chatty Ellie, just the soft sound of Harper talking. What was she telling her daughter?

He emerged, his hair finger-combed into place. Mia was waiting in the hall with Po in her arms. "Mommy says you're leaving." She gazed up at him sorrowfully.

"I can stay a few more minutes."

"I mean, you're moving right away. Not next summer like you said."

He wished Harper hadn't dropped that on her daughter. "Plans can change," he told her. "It isn't carved in stone."

"Does that mean no guarantees?" she asked.

"Kind of." Beyond Mia, Harper appeared. "We should talk some more," Peter told her.

"Not today."

Rather than argue in front of her daughter, he followed her to the living room, where he picked up the agent's message from the floor. "Keep this. I'll forward the email, as well."

Harper nodded. "Thanks for contacting her."

"I'm serious about—"

"Not now." Her uplifted palm stopped him.

His instincts urged him to fight for her. But a woman had a right to say no.

Mia trailed Peter to the front door like a small, sad ghost. Although he longed to reassure her, what could he say?

"This isn't the end," he told Harper, and would have embraced Mia except for the kitten in her arms. "Bye, sweetie."

"Peter?" Mia said.

"What, little one?"

Wheels must be turning in her head. "I guess you have to go because you were married to an angel and your children will be perfect, too. Not like me."

"That isn't true at all." He leaned down, bringing his face close to hers. "You're perfect to me."

"Not perfect enough." With that, she turned and scampered away, Po clinging to her shoulder.

Distressed, he regarded Harper. "She's taking it personally."

"This is what I was trying to avoid." From her guarded expression, Peter saw that she'd withdrawn somewhere he couldn't reach.

Not now, at least. He'd give her a few days and then they'd hash this out.

IT WASN'T FAIR. JUST when Harper had opened her heart to Peter, he'd sprung that news on her. An accelerated departure—but why not? Since she didn't plan to undergo another egg donation cycle, he had no reason to stick around.

He'd hired her as her donor, not as his girlfriend, but she'd yielded to her impulses. Why did she have to be a sucker for a sexy guy with a likable manner? Now Mia was paying the price for Harper's weakness.

The little girl had gone to her room and closed the door. Harper could hear her mumbling to Po unhappily, although she couldn't make out all the words. "Babies…go away… he can't take us."

Mia had to learn, sooner or later, not to depend on men, but she was only seven. And Peter seemed so damn lovable.

Missing him only agitated Harper further. Against her better judgment, she'd started to depend on him emotionally. Craving his comfort, cherishing his smile, looking forward to the feel of his strong arms around her.

She had to keep him at bay. Like she should have done in the first place.

Since she wasn't able to vent her feelings on Peter, Harper fired up her laptop and addressed an email to her long-silent brother. "Stop focusing on yourself and reach out to the people who love you," she wrote and, for good measure, added, "You moron."

She nearly deleted the insult, but he deserved it. Feeling a little better, she hit Send.

ALL WEEK, PETER'S CALLS to Harper went to voice mail, and weren't returned. In response to an email asking to meet this weekend, she replied tersely that she was tied up.

If only she'd help him sort this out. With Angela, when Peter had been unsure how to handle matters, she'd quietly provided guidance. Now he was on his own, and not doing terribly well.

He kept trying, without luck, to understand how he'd sabotaged their closeness. Should he have saved the news about his possibly accelerated departure? But eventually he'd have had to tell Harper, and she'd have been even angrier, with good reason.

He knew one thing: he loved her and her daughter. Yet

he also felt as if, by making love to Harper, he'd cheated on his wife. Everywhere he looked in his house, smiling figurines and cherished collector plates reminded him that this was her home, and that he'd promised to love her always.

The strain of transitioning to teaching P.E. didn't help, Peter reflected Thursday night as he reviewed his lesson plans at the kitchen table. California's standards were complex and, while well-intentioned in building healthy habits among students, frustrating, as well.

Requirements such as "discuss the changing psychological and sociological needs of a diverse society in relation to physical activity" and "recognize the value of physical activity in understanding multiculturalism" must sound great to some legislator. Implementing those with a bunch of hormone-fueled adolescents was another matter.

He sighed and returned to his work.

When the phone rang, his heart skittered. Could Harper be returning his calls at last?

Then he saw the name on the readout: Vanessa Ayres. Peter nearly stopped breathing. *Don't get your hopes up.* But when there was bad news, her husband had placed the call. Did this mean…?

"Peter," he answered, barely squeezing out his name.

"It's Vanessa. My test is positive!" Her voice brimmed with happiness. "And my hormones are raring to go. I'm eating dry crackers already." She spoke as if they were a special treat.

"You're pregnant?" Well, obviously, that was what the positive test results meant.

"I realize it's early, but this feels right," she said. "Like we're settled in for the long haul."

"That's fantastic. Do you need anything?" Words tumbled over one another. "What can I do?"

"Inhale," she advised.

"Good thing I'm sitting down." Even as Peter obeyed, his thoughts went on racing. A baby. Or babies. How incredible. "Does Harper know?"

"I plan to phone her next, unless you'd rather do it."

"You should contact her." *Considering that she isn't taking my calls.* "I'm sure she'll have questions."

"Good point. Well, then, I'll…" Vanessa broke off. "Oh, I nearly forgot. There've been two other pregnancies in the program this month, and we're planning a party tomorrow—5:00 p.m. at the hospital multipurpose room. Cake and punch. You're welcome to attend."

Peter had no after-school commitments, but if he promised to be there and Vanessa relayed the news, it might spook Harper. "I'll try to make it. Thanks for the invite. And the wonderful news. And for carrying my child. Children. Or both." He laughed. "That didn't make sense."

"I'm tickled pink." Vanessa chuckled. "What an old-fashioned term. It was one of my mom's favorites."

"Must be lucky, then."

After they signed off, Peter sat reveling in this wonderful news. And yearning to share the joy with Harper.

"I'LL SEE YOU AT THE party," Zack Sargent told Harper when they passed each other in the corridor at lunchtime on Friday. The doctor who'd performed both the egg extraction and the transfer didn't try to hide his satisfaction.

Harper merely nodded. Although she was happy for Peter, pleased for the program and overjoyed for the little boys in her dreams, she'd rather pick up Mia from day care and head home. And avoid the likelihood of running into the man she'd been ducking all week.

When Vanessa had said he'd try to attend, the surrogate had sounded doubtful. Harper, however, had read between the lines. He meant to be there, for certain; he just didn't want to scare her off.

Well, too bad. Her emotions had been on a roller-coaster ride since Sunday. Much as she'd like to celebrate with Una, Stacy, Vanessa and two other new moms-to-be, she'd rather not subject herself to seeing him.

And longing for him. And hurting all over again.

"See you at the party," Keely Randolph told her a few hours later. The older nurse was leaving in midafternoon, Paige having gone home earlier as scheduled.

"You're coming back for it?" Harper asked in surprise.

"Wouldn't miss it!"

Giving her a vague smile, Harper went to prep the next patient.

At four-thirty, she noted that Nora was running ahead of schedule, due to a couple of cancellations. Too bad, since having to stay at the office would have given Harper the perfect excuse not to go.

Her phone vibrated. The hallway was quiet and, seeing Stacy's name, Harper answered.

"Big news!" announced her friend, who'd returned two days ago from her honeymoon in Las Vegas. Cole, she'd reported, had acted like a kid in a candy shop. They'd taken in a show every night, and eaten each meal at a different hotel. He'd been so fascinated by the Venetian and the gondola ride in the canals that he was discussing taking a trip to Italy as soon as the triplets were old enough.

"Bigger news than Vanessa's and mine?" teased Harper.

"Of course not," her friend responded on cue. "But guess what! We found out the sex of the triplets."

That *was* important. "Well?" Harper prompted.

"Two boys and a girl!" Stacy reported. "If Vanessa is carrying two boys like you dreamed, we'll each have three kids of the same genders. Oh. Except you won't be raising them…that was tactless, wasn't it?"

"It's fine," Harper said. "Have you guys chosen names?"

"I'm working on it," Stacy said. "I will consider all reasonable suggestions."

"Doesn't Cole get a say?"

Her friend snorted. "A while ago, I suggested that he name any boys and I'd name any girls. You know what he came up with?"

Concerned about ignoring her duties, Harper peeked into the waiting room. Empty. Nora was in with a patient and didn't need her, either. "I'm afraid to ask."

"Groucho, Chico and Harpo," Stacy said. "Or maybe it was Curly, Moe and Larry."

"Larry's a good name." She didn't protest that Cole must have been joking when he suggested the names of the Marx Brothers, or the Three Stooges, either. With him, it was hard to tell.

Nora appeared in the hall. Harper had to see that the patient received all necessary instructions and prescriptions. "Duty calls."

"Wait! I have to a favor to ask." Stacy hurried on. "I brought my camera to get pictures of Cole and me and everybody because it's such a special day. The last time I asked somebody to do the honors, they cut off the tops of our heads. Nobody composes a shot like you do. Please, please, please will you take our pictures?"

Harper had no excuse for refusing and, besides, she hated to disappoint her friend. "Sure."

"Great! See you in a few minutes. Bye."

"Bye." There went Harper's chance of ducking out.

A short while later, she sent that patient and one more, the last of the day, home with their paperwork. Through the open door of Nora's office, she saw the doctor set down her cell phone. "How's Neo?" Harper asked. The toddler had been fussy this morning, and the doctor had been checking in with the hospital's day care center all day, in case a fever developed.

"He cut a tooth," she responded with obvious relief. "Are we finished?"

"We are," Harper confirmed. "I just have a few more details to take care of."

The obstetrician arose gracefully. "I'll see you at the party, then."

So much for fighting the inevitable. "See you at the party," Harper said.

Chapter Seventeen

Vanessa greeted Peter warmly. "I never expected this big a celebration!" The surrogate gestured toward a buffet table featuring trays of vegetables and cheeses, as well as small cakes. Pink and blue streamers draped the boxy room, which was filling up with people.

After a hard day at school, Peter was starving, but he ignored the food. He'd just spotted Harper training a camera on a group.

Out of courtesy, he checked his eagerness to rush over there. "How're you feeling?" he asked Vanessa.

"Healthy and heavy," she responded.

"Heavy, already?"

"Don't forget, in pregnancy the body forms an entirely new organ, the placenta," she said. "Or maybe two or three of them."

He wasn't sure how to answer that. A multiple pregnancy, while treasured, might pose problems for her health. Her husband, Tommy, saved Peter from answering by shaking his hand. A bank manager, the man wore a tailored suit that made Peter feel underdressed in slacks and a polo shirt. Still, he looked a lot better than an hour ago, before he'd showered and changed out of his exercise clothes.

"Congratulations, Dad," Tommy said with a grin.

Dad. What a fantastic nickname. "Thanks, for everything," Peter responded.

A dark-haired woman approached and introduced herself as Jennifer Martin. "Aren't you the public relations director?" Vanessa asked. "We have you to thank for the food and all."

"My pleasure." Shaking hands, the newcomer introduced them to the hospital administrator, Dr. Mark Rayburn, a powerfully built man who added his good wishes. For Peter, however, this was far from a first meeting. Dr. Rayburn, who still practiced medicine in addition to his business duties, had been Angela's ob-gyn.

"I'm glad to see you here under such happy circumstances," he told Peter.

"It's good to see you, too." He tried to erase the image of this kindly fellow, eyes filled with sorrow as he revealed the results of Angela's tests. The diagnosis had doomed her to an agonizing spiral of surgery, chemotherapy and radiation, all of which had failed to save her.

Harper, Peter noticed, remained on the far side of the room, taking more photographs. Whether by accident or design, she failed to glance in his direction.

Finally, his small group drifted off to greet others. When Peter spotted Harper again, she was navigating toward an exit.

He circled a trio of nurses, hoping to cut her off, even if it meant a spot of awkwardness. Although he had no brilliant game plan, perhaps, in person, she'd find it hard to refuse his request that they talk.

In his peripheral vision, a shimmer of pink appeared and then, for an instant, Angela's sweet face, drawn with suffering. Peter broke stride.

The woman strolling past bore only a passing resemblance to his late wife. But the mistaken identity had delayed him long enough for Harper to vanish.

Not again. Since the first day of sports camp, when he encountered Harper in the gym, he'd been imagining he glimpsed Angela at every turn. What was going on?

Adrienne halted alongside. "You look confused."

"Frustrated," he corrected. "It's the damnedest thing."

"What's that?"

"I keep thinking I see my wife." He hoped he didn't sound delusional.

"The one who died?"

"She's the only one I've got."

The doctor folded her arms and studied him. "Any particular timing to these visions?"

"Timing?" he inquired.

"Emotional occasions like this one," Adrienne said. "Your surrogate is pregnant, and Harper…" She glanced around. "Well, she *was* here."

"I was trying to catch up with her," Peter admitted.

"Any other connections to this hospital?"

There were, of course. "Her cancer was diagnosed here." He indicated Dr. Rayburn. "By him."

Adrienne gave one of those understanding nods that doctors must learn in medical school. "Have you talked to a counselor about survivor's guilt?"

Peter swallowed. "Like soldiers feel when their comrades are killed and they're still alive?"

"Precisely."

About to shrug off the idea, he paused. "I've never felt the need for counseling. Grief is natural."

"So is pain," she said. "We still take medicine for it."

Peter reflected for a moment. "I don't see why it would wait until two years after her death to hit me."

"Perhaps because you're starting to care about someone else?" Adrienne speculated.

He dredged up a recent observation. "I have felt like I'm cheating on her."

"When you deal with your guilt, you'll stop having visions," she said. "Now, my apologies, but I have to get back to Labor and Delivery. Congratulations, by the way."

"Thanks." Peter stuck around a while longer, to be civil and because he couldn't resist the food. Then he went home to think about Adrienne's words.

HARPER TRIED TO PAY close attention to her driving and to Mia's chatter about the day's events. No use. She could feel a flush of embarrassment stealing up her cheeks all the way home.

She'd fled the party to avoid Peter. She didn't want her friends, or him, to see how hurt she was.

This should have been their celebration together. Sure, there were issues to be resolved, and not easy ones, either. But they'd made love and she'd given him her heart. Although she'd been aware of his plans to leave, next summer had seemed far away, with the lingering possibility that he might change his mind. Then, just as they reached a new level of closeness, he'd admitted he was moving much sooner.

Being a decent guy, he'd tried to reach her this week. But she wasn't ready to act gracious. Okay, she'd donated her eggs and promised not to try to claim the baby, and she'd stand by that. But her self-control extended only so far.

If she burst into tears in front of everyone…well, she refused to do that. Harper had her pride. And her goals. To live independently, to enjoy seeing the world through her own eyes and her camera lens instead of molding her interests to a man's.

She'd lost sight of that, perhaps because she and Peter shared an enthusiasm for creating the picture book. Thanks to him, she was on track to receive professional photo credits and earn money for her photography, something she'd barely dared to dream of.

Had there been a chance for them? She could never be his ideal woman. Never turn into Angela, sweet and subtle. Harper was outspoken, direct and impulsive.

At home, as she fixed dinner, everything reminded her of him: the hummingbirds hovering around the patio feeder, the letter from the agent still sitting on a side table and, most of all, Mia's wilted air.

"I miss sports camp," the little girl said while they ate.

Although Harper took this as an indirect reference to Peter, she pretended otherwise. "Don't you like being in Mrs. Humphreys's class?"

"Sure I do." Distracted, the little girl described their latest lesson about California wildlife, from skunks and raccoons to coyotes and mountain lions. "We're writing stories about them for Back to School Night."

"That sounds like fun."

"And she wants me to teach the class how to make books, like Peter showed us."

There he was again. How long would it take for Mia's memories of him to fade?

As for Harper's memories, a perverse part of her didn't want them to fade. She valued the parts of herself he'd awakened, sexually and creatively. And she cherished his touch, his voice, his laughter. If he called again, she decided to hear him out.

While she was cleaning up, the phone rang. Her spirits lifting, Harper answered without checking the read-out. "Hi."

"Hey there, Harp." The gruff male voice—definitely not Peter's—caught her off guard. When she didn't reply, he added, "It's your brother, Jake. Are you mad?"

"Just surprised." Carrying the phone into the living room, Harper curled up on the sofa. "Did I guilt you into this?"

"Scared me, to tell the truth." Judging by his tone, he was only half kidding.

"Oh, come on."

"I had nightmares about my kid sister flying to New Mexico on her broomstick and casting me into the outer darkness," her brother joked. "And I'd deserve it."

"Yes, you would." But she'd already scolded him in her email. "How are you?"

"Better."

"Better than what?" She wished this were a video call. For now, she contented herself with a mental image of her brother: six feet tall, honey-brown hair, a few acne scars.

"Tough question."

Harper rephrased it. "How are you better?"

"I've changed a lot this past year, since I joined AA." He let out a long breath. "I got tired of being angry all the time."

"Who were you angry at?"

"At Dad for shutting me out, at the army because they didn't put me into combat. I thought that would help vent my feelings—stupid, huh? And, I'm ashamed to say, angry at Mom for dying when she was all I had to hold on to."

"Don't I count?" Harper protested.

"You're my little sister," her brother said. "I'm the one who's supposed to protect *you*. And I let you down."

"You moron."

He chuckled. "I'm glad you called me that in your email. I felt like you were right here in the room, reading me the riot act. It reminded me how much I like being around you. And that I owe you an apology. I'm sorry for running away and ignoring your messages."

"Apology accepted." She'd never felt that Jake owed her anything.

"You don't have to."

"Quit arguing."

"Yes, ma'am," he said lightly. "By the way, I accepted your friend request today. Love the pictures of Mia and her kitten. I can't wait to see them in person."

"Really?" He hadn't visited in the five years since their mother's death. Mia had been a toddler then. "Can we expect a visit?"

"For Thanksgiving, if you'll have me," Jake said. "I can take a few days off work, and I'll be on vacation from school."

"Of course we'll have you!" Mentally, Harper was already putting sheets on the spare bed. "And what's this about school?"

After years as a computer repairman, he explained, he'd decided to earn a degree in computer science. Juggling a part-time job and classes, he'd completed two years of undergraduate work.

"That's great." She'd feared her brother might wander through the years without direction, possibly ending up homeless. "You could have let me know."

"Your message was a much-needed kick in the pants," he said. "I'm afraid I inherited the family tendency to push people away."

"What family tendency?"

"Being afraid to let people see how vulnerable we are," Jake answered. "I learned that from my sponsor at AA.

The more we love someone, the more scared we are of revealing our deepest emotions and being hurt. That's the way we grew up, or I did, anyway."

"Mom never pushed us away," Harper replied, puzzled.

"No, but Dad did. I think that's why he filled every spare minute with activities." Her brother cleared his throat. "I needed his approval, and instead he rejected me. Or that's how it seemed. In retrospect, I guess he took my adolescent lashing-out as a rejection of *him*."

"Your relationship was complicated," Harper agreed. "By the way, your niece just walked into the room."

Mia paused, a board game tucked under one arm. "Is that Uncle Jake?"

"It is," she confirmed.

"Put her on!" Jake said eagerly.

Mia took the phone, and soon was chattering about Po and school. "We brought our favorite stuffed animals the first day and Mrs. Humphreys took our picture," she told him. "It's on the class website."

Marveling at how readily the girl opened up to her uncle, Harper sat on the arm of a chair, mulling Jake's comment. *She* didn't have a tendency to push people away. If she'd done that to Peter today, she'd had good reason: he'd done it to her, first.

Hadn't he?

She tried to recall what he'd told her while they were lying in bed. To her, it had sounded like a declaration that he planned to leave her behind. But in retrospect, she wasn't sure he'd said that.

The pain had cut so deep, she hadn't probed further. Now, she recalled that he'd only learned the previous day about his parents' home selling.

Then he'd called and emailed, trying to get together. She'd assumed he only meant to smooth things over in the short run, before letting her down easy, as if such a thing were possible.

Today at the hospital, she'd seen him watching her. When she slipped out, Harper had expected him to follow, and been troubled that he didn't, despite the fact that she'd intended to brush him off.

How ridiculous. She was acting like a teenager. *Trying to protect myself,* just as her brother had said, but family tendency or not, she loved Peter. He deserved a chance to show that he loved her.

If he confirmed her fears, she'd survive. It was a risk worth taking.

With that resolution, Harper reclaimed the phone and resumed her conversation with her brother.

Chapter Eighteen

That afternoon was the first time Peter brought silk flowers to the cemetery. They lasted longer than fresh, a prospect that had always deterred him because it would imply that he meant to visit less often.

A half-dozen rows off, someone had erected a large floral display at what he presumed was the site of a scheduled burial, but no one had arrived yet. Standing on the clipped green expanse near Angela's plaque, he was grateful for the absence of other visitors.

He was alone. They could talk.

"I'm not abandoning you," he told Angela as he settled the bouquet of peach-colored roses and white calla lilies in the new vase. His wife would have loved these hues. Peach had flattered her pale complexion and hazel eyes. Today, her features stood out in his mind because he'd been watching a DVD of her.

She wasn't an angel figurine or a vague, floating memory. She'd been a real woman who'd died much too young, at twenty-nine.

"There's a special place in my heart that will always belong to you," Peter told her. "You were my first love. But I have to move on."

He'd wept during the video of their wedding and other happy occasions. Then, after it ended, he'd yielded to memories of her last days, which until now he'd tried to think about as little as possible. There were no photos, intentionally, and he'd told himself it was kinder to picture the healthy, vital Angela, not the suffering cancer patient.

But he'd suppressed those images for his own sake, he realized.

In the final months, his health and strength had contrasted painfully with her frailty. Frustrated, he'd tried to use his strength to save her. He'd researched and applied to clinical trials under way in Southern California, driving her to test facilities as long as she was able, but either she hadn't fit the parameters or they'd been too early or too late. Time had run out. If only he'd worked harder, scoured the internet and flown her to another state…

Peter shook his head. Most likely, he'd have accomplished nothing except to increase Angela's suffering. Her disease had caught them both by surprise, with its hideous onslaught and rapid progression. It was no one's fault.

Last night, he'd finally acknowledged what bound him so tightly to his late wife: not the sweet ties of romantic love, but useless, unreasonable guilt.

"I love someone else," he told Angela. "Not more than you and not less. I don't even know if Harper loves me back, but I'm ready to say goodbye to you on this earth."

A lump in his throat blocked further words. He had nothing left to give.

On the driveway, a car stopped near his. A middle-aged couple in dark clothing emerged. The family for today's burial, perhaps. Peter's heart went out to them. He hoped they were burying someone who'd succumbed after a long and fulfilling span of years.

The kind of long, fulfilling life he hoped to lead with Harper.

Regret and sorrow held him in place a moment longer,

but he heard more cars pulling up. With a bittersweet mixture of regret and relief, he turned away. As he walked, he seemed to feel Mia's little hand in his, comforting him.

With a burst of determination, he decided to stop at a special place on the way home. Then he'd take his chances with the living, breathing woman he loved.

SHE SHOULD HAVE CONTACTED Peter in advance, Harper thought as she rang his doorbell for the third time. How silly to expect him to be sitting at home on a sunny Saturday. He might be coaching students, or out for a run on the beach, or grocery shopping.

She'd decided this morning to stop by, skipping awkward explanations over the phone. Luckily, he'd included his street address on his email to the agent.

She'd appealed to her neighbor Caroline for emergency babysitting. The young woman had reacted with an immediate yes, claiming Mia would be a big help to her and her mother in making persimmon jam.

"Our tree's overloaded," she'd said. "The more hands, the faster it'll go. Relax and have fun, whatever you're doing."

"Just visiting a friend," Harper had replied. "I owe you a favor."

"Not at all," Caroline had said. "There's one condition, though."

"What's that?" Harper had asked, more out of curiosity than because of any reluctance.

"You have to take home half a dozen jars. There's always far more than we can use."

"You bet." Mia would be thrilled to eat jam she'd helped prepare.

Harper stepped back for another look at the cottage's fairy-tale-style gingerbread trim and latticed windows.

Suppose Peter was in the backyard? But venturing into the side yard to peer over the fence would mean spying on him.

Instead, she took out her phone. Might as well try to reach him wherever he was, and ask when he'd be available. She didn't have to admit that she'd foolishly rushed over, unannounced.

Her finger was hovering over his contact number when his van pulled into the driveway. Well, that settled that, she mused with a touch of embarrassment, and put away the phone.

As Peter got out, uncertainty clouded his expression. "Did we have an appointment?"

"No. I'm being pushy," Harper said.

The edges of his mouth twitched. "Push all you like."

As Peter cut across the lawn to her, she caught her breath. How touchable and solid he looked, and how well she remembered the curve of his mouth as it claimed hers.

Harper nearly reached out for a hug, until she spotted the small sack in one of his hands. The other held his keys. She could picture them fumbling, dropping things and generally entertaining any neighbors who might be watching.

"Glad to see you aren't tied up, after all," he said.

"Tied up?"

"You said you were busy today," he reminded her.

"Oh, uh, my plans changed." That was true, as far as it went.

"So you came over...?" he prompted.

"Yes, but I thought you were out," she said. "And you were. But now you're home. Which is good. Unless you're busy." *Oh, Harper, stop yammering.*

"Nope." He unlocked the door.

Inside, dust and traces of a flowery perfume tickled her nose. Harper sneezed.

"Catching a cold?" Peter asked.

"I'm fine." But she wasn't. In dismay, Harper stared at the large display cabinets, their doors open and shelves half-empty. Clean spaces showed where items had been removed, no doubt similar to the figurines and decorative plates still in evidence. On the carpet, wrapped objects filled cardboard boxes, with rolls of bubble wrap and empty boxes waiting.

This wasn't the house of a man undecided about his plans. "You're moving already." Her voice quavered.

"What? No." Peter's keys rattled. He stuck them in his pocket.

Harper frowned at the disordered living room. "What's all this, then?"

"There's a store called A Memorable Decor that will take this stuff on consignment," he explained. "I plan to donate the proceeds to cancer research."

Generous, and sensible. "That way you don't have to move this across the country," Harper concluded. "I love that store, by the way."

"I should have offered you these things," he said.

"No, thanks." She tilted her head. "They aren't my style."

"They aren't mine, either." He seemed to be searching for words. "Hold on a minute."

Peter ducked into the hallway, returning a moment later with a large windowed box containing a wedding dress. "The proprietor offered to sell this for me, too, but I'd rather donate it. I found an organization that gives gently used bridal gowns to the families of marines." Camp Pendleton, a major marine training base, was located just south of Orange County.

"How lovely." Harper wrapped her arms around herself. "I gave away my wedding dress. I'm sure Mia will want to pick her own."

"No doubt."

The room fell silent. They'd never been at a loss for words before, Harper realized. "I guess I'm interrupting your packing."

"Not really," Peter said. "I was hoping to see you."

Harper dredged up her excuse for coming. "I brought my latest shots of hummingbirds. Maybe we could propose a second book after we finish this one."

"I'd like that very much. But first…" He touched her arm lightly and drew back. How strange to be shy with each other, after they'd made love with such urgency, Harper thought. "Come outside with me for a minute."

"Sure," she said. He must want to show her the yard. Was he redoing that, too?

Still carrying the small sack, he guided her through the house. It was slightly larger than her rental, with appealing feminine touches everywhere except the rear bedroom, which had been converted to a den. From the hall, Harper noted the dark desk, padded chairs and small TV set. "That must be your retreat."

"It is," he confirmed. "Although I expect to hang out more in the front room once it's furnished with a large-screen. Maybe one as big as yours."

"Sean bought that." Wryly, she added, "I don't plan to donate it to charity, however."

"That would be criminal," he retorted. "Unless you could borrow it back during football season."

"You mean ice-skating season."

"That, too."

Emerging into the backyard, Harper caught her breath at the beauty of the design. A meandering walkway led between gorgeous roses in shades of white, pink, coral and red. White alyssum edged the beds. A honeysuckle-draped arbor led to a gazebo shaded by an orange tree.

"It's gorgeous." She inhaled the scents of roses and mint, grateful for the fresh air after the dusty house. "How can you bear to leave this place?"

"It isn't the place that matters." Peter's voice rasped with an unfamiliar hoarseness.

"I suppose not." A *whoom* drew Harper's attention to a tiny jewel-colored bird hovering at a trumpet-shaped honeysuckle blossom. "You don't need a feeder. This is a natural hummer habitat."

"I could add a feeder, too. Then we'd have even more of them."

We? She kept sensing an undercurrent of tension in Peter. Was that due to her barging in unannounced? But he'd said he wanted to see her. "I'm sorry I've been avoiding you. I may have jumped to conclusions about your plans."

"Apparently so."

"I'm willing to listen, if you're willing to talk," Harper said.

He hesitated. "Actions speak louder than words."

Was he upset with her? "I don't understand."

He indicated a white wrought-iron bench. "Mind having a seat?"

She complied, finding the bench comfortable despite its hard surfaces. Belatedly, she wondered if she should have checked for dust, but soiled clothing was the least of her concerns.

Peter glanced at the sack. It was elegant, silver foil stripes alternating with textured white. Fancy chocolates? Harper wondered. But that would hardly account for his nervousness.

"Brace yourself," he said.

"I'm sitting down," she reminded him.

"I guess that was more for my benefit than yours," he

said with an apologetic smile, and then he did something extraordinary.

He went down on one knee.

PETER DIDN'T REMEMBER being anywhere near this anxious when he proposed to Angela. His heart hadn't stuck in his throat, and his pulse hadn't sped as if he'd just run a mile. Of course, he hadn't been worried that she might reject him, either.

Seeing Harper in his house had transformed it into a place of new possibilities where they could raise Mia and their baby or babies-to-be, sharing decisions, supporting and encouraging each other. He needed her, and loved her so much that he couldn't imagine her not feeling the same way.

But there were, as Mia might say, no guarantees.

Still, she'd come here, and there she sat, awaiting his next words with her lips parted and her eyes bright. What a unique spirit she had, this woman who had healed Peter's heart.

From the sack, he retrieved a velvet box and lifted the hinged lid. Sunlight caught the diamond, awakening its brilliant clarity along with the gleam of sapphires on either side. He wished he'd prepared more carefully for this moment. And that he saw more in her face than simple astonishment.

Go for it. "Harper, will you marry me?" Peter asked.

She swallowed.

He let his thoughts spill out, unguarded. "I love you. Let's make a home, you and me and our children. You can pursue your photography. I'll handle the baby care. Well, as much as possible. And, um—" what had he left out? "—we can exchange the ring if you'd prefer a different one."

He hadn't spoken eloquently, but he'd been honest. Was it enough?

"The ring's exquisite." Her chest rose and fell. "But I know how much you want to move back East to be with your family. It might be hard on Mia to leave her friends...." The tip of her tongue flicked over dry lips. "Oh, heck, what's so terrible about starting over?"

"We'll stay here." Peter had no qualms on that score. "The point is to surround the baby with a loving family. If you'll marry me, we'll do that."

She leaned forward, her fingers tracing his jawline. "But your job's making you miserable."

"There are other schools in Southern California," he said. "And till I find the right one, I can put up with teaching P.E."

"What about your parents?"

"They'll adjust." Peter gave a dry chuckle, still uncertain of her response. "When—if—we get married, do you suppose we'll debate everything?"

"We do both have strong personalities," Harper said. "Is that a problem?"

"Not if you're saying yes," he answered, and rubbed his cheek against her hand. "Frankly, I like hashing things out. That way, we reach solutions that suit us both."

"I love you, Peter." Harper's forehead touched his. "The answer is yes."

Around them, the world buzzed and hummed with joy. How lonely he'd been these past two years, and how easily Harper had lifted that burden.

He was going to be her husband. And Mia's father. And they were having a baby, too. Incredible.

Peter kissed her lightly, which was the best he could manage from this position. Then he sat beside her and slipped the ring onto her finger. It was a little loose, but fixable.

Harper nestled against him. "There's a basketball court," she said.

"What?" Peter wondered if he'd misheard.

Her laughter tinkled through the air. "Around the corner of the house. I couldn't see it before."

Now he understood. "I'm full of surprises."

"You are, indeed." Harper slid her arm around his waist, and they kissed again, for a long, thrilling time.

When they reluctantly broke off, she said, "It might seem a little strange."

"What might?" Peter asked, too delirious to think straight.

"There seems to be a trend toward pregnant brides." She released a mock sigh. "But in our case, we're having a baby that I'm not carrying. How will that look? Will we be snubbed by wedding planners?"

"You could wear a padded pillow."

"I just might." Harper rested her head on his shoulder. "Mia will love being a flower girl."

He wrapped his arm around her. "I hope she'll love having a daddy."

"More than you can imagine."

Peter could imagine it. With Harper in his arms, he could imagine a lot of things.

Most of all, a future full of happiness.

Chapter Nineteen

"Are you ready?" After applying her lipstick, Harper peered from her bathroom to see Mia twirling in front of the bedroom's full-length mirror. Her daughter had changed from new jeans and a top into the dress she'd worn to Stacy's wedding. "Honey, that's too fancy for lunch."

"It isn't lunch, it's high tea!" the little girl protested.

If Harper raised a fuss, it would only delay them further, she supposed, and Peter was due to arrive any minute. "All right. Let me brush your hair."

Mia held still. Knowing she had at best thirty seconds before her daughter started fidgeting, Harper ran her own brush through the little girl's pixie cut. It was adorable. How could anyone not fall in love with this child?

Considering the neglectful treatment she received from Sean's mother, Harper knew the answer to that. She just didn't like it.

In this case, though, the grandparents were strangers. It would be unreasonable to expect instant bonding. Still, surely they would put up a good pretense for Mia's sake.

Barely had the brush stopped moving than the little girl darted out of the room. All morning, she'd been working on a new minibook featuring pictures of her stuffed animals. She probably wanted to tweak that and print it out again.

As expected, Mia had leaped into Peter's arms when she learned he was to be her new daddy. Her cheers had rung through the house, scaring Po, whom they'd later found hiding under the bed.

For the past two weeks, Harper had been floating with happiness. She and Peter talked almost every night, and last weekend they'd found a chance to make love again. At work, she'd been inundated with congratulations.

Then, to everyone's delight, an ultrasound had revealed that Vanessa was carrying twins. While it was too soon to determine the gender, Harper had drawn up a list of boys' names to review with Peter. They were considering Rod, after his father, and Jacob, after hers, but also Van—in honor of Vanessa—plus a few more.

As for Mia, she was over the moon. "I'm going to have a daddy!" she announced to everyone they saw.

The excitement had shaded into nervousness a few days ago, however, when she learned she'd be meeting the elder Gladstones. "They won't really be my grandparents, will they?" she'd said.

"Sure they will." In honesty, Harper had added, "Step-grandparents."

"The twins will be their real grandchildren," she'd said. "And that baby in Maryland."

"Betty's daughter." Harper had told her about Peter's sister and her pregnancy.

"I wish they *were* my grandparents," Mia had said over breakfast this morning. Then she'd trotted off to prepare her book. While the Gladstones had of course included Mia in today's invitation, Harper hoped they'd hide any discomfort they felt about her neediness. She knew how perceptive her daughter was.

His parents had already expressed their welcome to

Harper over the phone. "Peter says wonderful things about you" was how his mother had put it when they spoke.

"It's kind of you to invite us to lunch," Harper had answered, unsure what else to say. That she loved their son? Obviously. That they must be terrific folks to have raised such a terrific guy? That might come across as false flattery. "Can I bring anything?"

"No, thanks," Kerry had replied. "I have a special menu planned. I've been researching my husband's heritage and it turns out Rod's ancestors were mostly Scottish. I'll be serving a Scottish-inspired high tea. It's actually lunch, but high tea sounds better."

"I can't wait." Celebrating one's ancestry did sound like fun. Harper's mother had told her once that she was part French with a Native American great-grandmother, but hadn't seemed to consider it important.

Returning her attention to the mirror, Harper studied her lavender blouse and gray skirt. Was this too conservative? Oh, seriously, it wasn't as if Peter's parents were sitting in judgment.

Her hair had grown to collar-length, and Harper decided to keep it that way. For her wedding, she might wear it loose, with a flower clipped in. Since this was her second marriage, she'd rather choose a dress she could wear again. Autumn colors would be lovely.

They'd set a tentative date for Thanksgiving weekend, so her brother could attend. After congratulating her wholeheartedly, Jake had happily agreed to give away the bride.

A yowl, more distressed than Po's usual meows, yanked Harper from her thoughts. "Mia, what are you doing to the cat?" She sped into the living room.

There sat the carrier they used for visits to the vet.

Inside, the black-and-white kitten—nearly full grown—turned around and around, searching for escape.

"He's coming with us," Mia announced.

Harper stared at her in disbelief. "What on earth gave you that idea?"

"They might not think I'm special but everybody loves Po," Mia said.

Harper reached out and drew her daughter close. "You are absolutely the most special little girl in the world. If they don't love you, they aren't worthy of Peter, because *he* loves you."

There was no answer.

Harper peered down. "Well?"

"I didn't really think you'd let me take Po." Wiggling away, Mia knelt to release the cat, which wasted no time in scampering off. "Sorry," she called after him.

Outside, a vehicle halted. "Got the book?" Harper asked.

With a shrug, her daughter brushed kitty hairs from her dress. "Yeah, I put it in a big envelope like you said."

Through the front window, Harper saw Peter striding up the walk. The sight of him drove out all other thoughts. He was just as handsome and exciting and sexy as when she'd seen him the first day of sports camp, which—she now conceded—was when she'd started falling in love.

In the doorway, his appreciative gaze went first to her, and then to Mia. "How're my girls?" he asked.

"One of them is so anxious she tried to bring her cat along," Harper answered.

"Mommy, he can tell you mean me!" Mia clutched the manila envelope. Harper hoped it would protect the book, because otherwise the pages would soon be creased into oblivion.

"Most cats don't like car rides," Peter reflected. "Where is he?"

"Hiding, no doubt." Harper picked up her purse. "Shall we?"

"After you, my lady." He held the door. "And my little lady."

Mia grinned. "Thank you, Daddy!"

She fell quiet in the van's rear seat and remained that way during the twenty-minute drive. Harper had to fight the temptation to keep turning and checking on her daughter. She couldn't force the child to relax, any more than she could calm her own nagging worry about the upcoming meeting.

Apparently keyed up, too, Peter drummed his fingers on the steering wheel as they exited the freeway in Yorba Linda. "You okay?" Harper asked.

"I heard something at school today." He'd gone in early on a Saturday to spend a few hours working with the track team. Just then, he had to swerve to miss a car pulling out of a parking lot. "Never mind—I'd better stay focused on my driving. We can talk about it later."

A couple of miles farther, they entered a residential neighborhood, the planned type with coordinated adobe exteriors, slight variations in size and shape and low-key landscaping. It was lovely, but Harper preferred the more diverse assortment of houses in Safe Harbor. They had more interesting shadows and angles for photographing.

As they swung into a cul-de-sac, Harper spotted a silver-haired man of about Peter's height and slightly heavier build deadheading roses in front of a two-story home. He peered up and waved.

"Your father came outside to greet us?" Harper said. "How thoughtful."

"And meanwhile, he's catching up on some neglected gardening," Peter observed wryly. "My dad never wastes a minute."

When they parked and got out, Harper found herself clasped in a hug, followed by a second one from Peter's mom. Wearing an apron that said, Kiss Me! Some of My Ancestors Are Irish, Kerry Gladstone had sped out to greet them, as well. With her curly hair and the laugh-crinkles around her eyes, she exuded goodwill.

Mia held back, lurking close to Peter. She stuck her hand in his for a moment, and then retrieved it. He glanced down, clearly concerned, but didn't say anything. Calling attention to her behavior might make her even more self-conscious.

We're all nervous, Harper mused as she followed Kerry, who was chattering about her internet search for recipes.

"I've met people who don't believe Scotland has much of a cuisine, but they're wrong," Kerry said, leading them through an airy, cathedral-ceilinged living room and into a sunny kitchen.

"Whatever you're fixing, it smells delicious." Harper drank in the aromas of butter, garlic and oranges.

"Cheese scones for sandwiches." Kerry indicated a tray filled with flaky rolls stuffed with what appeared to be cream cheese. "And for dessert, sherry and brandy trifle, without the sherry and brandy. I used orange juice and flavored syrup instead."

Mia stared around without speaking. At a soft brushing noise, she gazed eagerly into a corner of the room, but it was only the curtains at an open window. Not a pet, as Harper suspected she'd been hoping.

"We're eating on the patio." Kerry opened the glass sliding door. "Mia, will you help me serve?"

"Sure." Solemnly, the little girl reached for the large tray.

Peter's mother intervened smoothly. "That might be a bit heavy. How about bringing the forks and spoons?" She gave Mia a plastic holder, with a handle and open compartments filled with silverware.

Mia nodded. Moving with great care, she toted it outside.

Peter took the tray, while Rod carried the large salad bowl and Harper brought the dressing and salad tongs. "I'm impressed," she told her future mother-in-law as they took seats around a table on the flagstone terrace. "You're quite a cook."

"Thanks." Kerry beamed. "I love researching our backgrounds and fixing special foods. Of course, it's more enjoyable when we have people to share with."

"Your home is lovely, too."

"We like it." Intercepting a meaningful glance from his wife, Rod clamped his mouth shut.

What did that mean? Harper supposed they'd rather not talk about their upcoming move. It must be a sensitive topic.

They'd lavished care on this yard, from the whirlpool enclosure to the outdoor kitchen. With a grill, burners and a small refrigerator, it was perfect for whipping up treats for a crowd.

What a shame to leave it. But they'd made a sensible choice. In a few years, if Peter had no luck finding a job teaching science, Harper supposed he and she might decide to join them.

The discussion moved on to their daughter's pregnancy and Vanessa's ultrasound. When they'd exhausted those subjects, Harper asked about the ingredients of their meal. Kerry told them that the scones contained a Scottish cheddar along with sliced green onions. She'd used herbed Boursin cheese as a sandwich filling.

"Do you share recipes?" Harper asked. "I'd enjoy fixing this for my friends."

"Certainly," Kerry responded. "I'll email it to you."

"I'd appreciate that."

Through it all, Mia chewed slowly and carefully, which was unusual. Although she seemed to like the food, she didn't say anything.

Kerry studied her thoughtfully. The older woman didn't pressure the child to talk, though. As a retired elementary schoolteacher, she was clearly sensitive to children's moods.

Too bad only about a month remained before their escrow closed, Harper reflected. The Gladstones would be busy packing and moving. That didn't leave much time for getting acquainted.

For dessert, Kerry produced a baking sheet of pastry covered with whipped cream and toasted almonds. "This has a funny name—it's called a whim-wham."

Harper couldn't help smiling. Peter regarded his mother in amusement.

"Why?" Mia asked.

"The word used to mean something light and fanciful," Kerry explained. "Which describes this very well."

"What's in it?" Harper suspected she'd want the recipe for this, too.

"Beneath all the whipped cream are ladyfingers soaked in the orange juice and syrup."

"Ladyfingers? Ick!" Mia blinked as if startled by her own response. "I'm sorry. Can I un-ick that?"

Rod guffawed. The girl regarded him uncertainly.

Kerry chuckled. "You absolutely can un-ick that, Mia. In fact, I'll give you the first serving."

"Okay." The little girl sounded dubious. One bite, though, and her face lit up. "Yum!"

"There's enough for seconds." Kerry dished out the

rich dessert to everyone. As she resumed her seat, she said, "Mia, I'm hoping you can help me solve a problem."

Fork poised for another bite, the girl frowned. "What kind of problem?"

"My hobby is researching our family background," Kerry began.

"Geo…gea…gecology," Mia attempted.

The response was an approving nod. "You're close. Genealogy. I'll bet you're good at reading and writing."

"I take pictures, too." The little girl glanced at the envelope she'd placed on an empty chair but left it untouched.

"Unfortunately, I've run out of people to research," Kerry said.

Pleased at the approach the older woman was using, Harper concentrated on eating. Peter merely watched, his eyes sparkling.

"What about the baby in Maryland? She'll need gee-nee-ology." Mia pronounced each syllable distinctly.

"My son-in-law's parents hired a service to draw up their family tree." Kerry sounded disappointed. "So we already know about both sides of the baby's family, theirs and ours. The problem is, if I don't have anyone else to study, I can't find new recipes, either."

Having cleaned her plate, Mia set down her fork. "What about the twins?"

"We've got Peter pegged, but then there's your mom's side of the family." Kerry gave her husband a sideways glance.

"I have an idea," Rod said. "Harper's ancestors are Mia's, too. Maybe she could help you, Kerry." If his words had a rehearsed tone, Mia didn't seem to notice.

"I can do that!" She picked up the package. "See, I wrote a book. My stuffed animals are kind of like a family."

About to warn her not to use sticky fingers on the paper,

Harper clamped her mouth shut. They could always print another copy.

Peter's mother leafed through the booklet. "Wow. You did this yourself?"

"All of it," Mia confirmed.

"She's teaching her class how to make them," Harper put in. "And by the way, I think my ancestors were French and Native American."

"This is even better than I hoped." Kerry handed the book gently to her husband. "I'll interview you to find out as many facts as you can remember. Then Mia can help me on the computer. When we're done, we can make a book."

"And I'll read it to the twins!" Abruptly, Mia's face fell. "But we can't. You're going away."

"About that." Rod cleared his throat.

His wife picked up the cue. "Our house fell out of escrow."

"What's that mean?" Mia asked.

"That the sale won't go through," Peter said. "I'm sorry."

"We're not," they chorused.

Harper felt a swell of relief. Was it possible they might stay? "What went wrong?"

"The people who planned to buy our house didn't get their loan approved by the bank," Rod told them. "They'll qualify for a smaller house, though, so they can still find a nice place."

"It was a wake-up call," Kerry said. "I've been realizing how much we'll miss our friends."

"I'm not crazy about shoveling snow, either," added her husband.

Nearby, a bird began chirping. To Harper, the air smelled fresher and the grass looked greener.

"What about living near Betty?" Peter asked.

"We decided to buy a condo in Maryland and divide

our time," his father said. "It'll be a good investment, and that way we can enjoy all our grandchildren."

"All four of them." Kerry met Harper's gaze. "I hope our sticking around isn't a problem."

"Why would it be a problem?" Peter asked.

"Not every bride wants her in-laws underfoot, especially when she's been assured they're leaving."

"Mommy!" Mia said. "You won't chase them away, will you?"

Harper swallowed her astonishment. "Well, honey, if you really, really, really want to have grandparents..."

"Yes!" Mia bounced in her chair so hard that Peter and his father both grabbed the table to steady it.

"And you don't mind visiting them and doing all that hard work on the computer..." Harper felt the corners of her mouth twitching.

Kerry covered her smile with a napkin.

"I don't mind, Mommy," Mia said earnestly.

"Then I guess it's okay." Unable to contain herself any longer, Harper shared an understanding grin with her in-laws-to-be.

Mia folded her arms. "You're making fun of me."

"No, I'm teasing because you're so cute," Harper said.

"There's one thing we need to seal this deal." Kerry pushed back her chair. "That's a hug."

Mia flew out of her seat so fast, it was lucky both men were holding the table.

After a round of embraces, the little girl helped clear the dishes. Then Kerry brought out her tablet computer and showed Mia and Harper her favorite website.

"Let's save the research till we have more time," Kerry suggested after she'd demonstrated how the site worked. "Mia, you can interview your mommy about your grandparents and great-grandparents, and write it all down. That will give us a starting place."

"Right now!"

"Not today," Harper was saying when Peter emerged with his father from inside, where they'd been playing Ping-Pong. "Who won?"

"He did," Rod said gruffly. "But only because I ate too much for lunch. Slows me down."

Peter clapped his father on the back. "Don't worry. We'll have a rematch next time."

"I could teach you to play, Mia," Rod said.

"I bet I can beat you." She sprang to her feet. "Peter taught me at sports camp."

"Sports camp teaches children to play Ping-Pong?" The older man pretended to glare at his son. "Shouldn't you leave something for your elders to do?"

"She's pretty good, too," Peter said jovially.

"I was hoping there'd be one person in the family I could beat." Rod sighed. "We'll play next time, okay, Mia?"

"Sure!"

As Kerry put away the tablet, Harper rose to leave. Peter stopped her with a raised hand. "I nearly forgot."

"What's that?" she asked.

"This morning while I was coaching, one of my colleagues said he overheard Lidia Sakioka saying how much she hates teaching biology." To the others, he explained, "She's the Japanese teacher who bumped me."

"Yes, but what's she going to do about it?" his father queried.

Peter's eyebrows quirked. "She might take early retirement. Keep your fingers crossed. If she does, I could be back in my old classroom next fall instead of teaching P.E."

Everyone applauded, except Mia. "Won't you still teach sports camp?"

Peter patted her shoulder. "Sure I will. That's a different job entirely."

She gave a joyful hop. "Good!"

Soon afterward, they left for home. In the backseat, Mia dozed off. Although it was only midafternoon, she'd had an intense day.

Harper's eyelids felt heavy, too, so she rested them for a moment. The next thing she knew, they were passing a familiar green field. Daisies flourished and butterflies danced, and two little boys were playing catch with a shadowy figure.

Then she saw him clearly. It was Peter, pitching the ball and calling encouragement. He wasn't alone. As if by magic, his father had become part of the game, while his mother and Mia folk-danced in a circle. Then Harper wasn't standing back watching anymore. She was out there laughing and joining the fun.

It might be only a dream. But as she blinked into wakefulness, Harper knew that some dreams really did come true.

Like this one.

* * * * *

REQUEST YOUR FREE BOOKS!
2 FREE NOVELS PLUS 2 FREE GIFTS!

HARLEQUIN®
American ★ Romance®
LOVE, HOME & HAPPINESS

YES! Please send me 2 FREE Harlequin® American Romance® novels and my 2 FREE gifts (gifts are worth about $10). After receiving them, if I don't wish to receive any more books, I can return the shipping statement marked "cancel." If I don't cancel, I will receive 4 brand-new novels every month and be billed just $4.74 per book in the U.S. or $5.24 per book in Canada. That's a savings of at least 14% off the cover price! It's quite a bargain! Shipping and handling is just 50¢ per book in the U.S. and 75¢ per book in Canada.* I understand that accepting the 2 free books and gifts places me under no obligation to buy anything. I can always return a shipment and cancel at any time. Even if I never buy another book, the two free books and gifts are mine to keep forever.

154/354 HDN F4YN

Name	(PLEASE PRINT)

Address	Apt. #

City	State/Prov.	Zip/Postal Code

Signature (if under 18, a parent or guardian must sign)

Mail to the Harlequin® Reader Service:
IN U.S.A.: P.O. Box 1867, Buffalo, NY 14240-1867
IN CANADA: P.O. Box 609, Fort Erie, Ontario L2A 5X3

Want to try two free books from another line?
Call 1-800-873-8635 or visit www.ReaderService.com.

* Terms and prices subject to change without notice. Prices do not include applicable taxes. Sales tax applicable in N.Y. Canadian residents will be charged applicable taxes. Offer not valid in Quebec. This offer is limited to one order per household. Not valid for current subscribers to Harlequin American Romance books. All orders subject to credit approval. Credit or debit balances in a customer's account(s) may be offset by any other outstanding balance owed by or to the customer. Please allow 4 to 6 weeks for delivery. Offer available while quantities last.

Your Privacy—The Harlequin® Reader Service is committed to protecting your privacy. Our Privacy Policy is available online at www.ReaderService.com or upon request from the Harlequin Reader Service.

We make a portion of our mailing list available to reputable third parties that offer products we believe may interest you. If you prefer that we not exchange your name with third parties, or if you wish to clarify or modify your communication preferences, please visit us at www.ReaderService.com/consumerschoice or write to us at Harlequin Reader Service Preference Service, P.O. Box 9062, Buffalo, NY 14269. Include your complete name and address.

HAR13R

Looking for another great Western read?
Read on for a sneak peek of

THE RANCHER'S HOMECOMING

by Cathy McDavid

July's Harlequin
Recommended Read!

*Annie Hennessee has her hands full with
rebuilding the Sweetheart Inn following a
devastating forest fire. But what is Sam Wyler
doing back in town? Isn't it enough that he
broke Annie's heart all those years ago?*

A figure emerged from the shadows. A man. He wore jeans and
boots, and a black cowboy hat was pulled low over his brow.

Even so, she instantly recognized him, and her broken heart
beat as if it was brand-new.

Sam! He was back. After nine years.

Why? And what was he doing at the Gold Nugget?

"Annie?" He started down the stairs, the confused expression
on his face changing to one of recognition. "It's you!"

Suddenly nervous, she retreated. If he hadn't seen her, she'd
have run.

No, that was a stupid reaction. She wasn't young and vulnerable
anymore. She was thirty-four. The mother of a three-year-old
child. Grown. Confident. Strong.

And yet the door beckoned. He'd always had that effect on her,
been able to strip away her defenses.

A rush of irritation, more at herself than him, galvanized her.